FROM THE
NANCY DREW FILES

THE CASE: Nancy's investigation into a kidnapping is going nowhere; if only she could read minds . . .

CONTACT: Nancy has worked with police captain Philip Krane before, but this time she's looking for his daughter, Sharon.

SUSPECTS: Tommy Rio—Sharon Krane's boyfriend had an argument with her at a party; did he decide to win the fight at any cost?

Eddie Hill—Captain Krane put him behind bars. Now that he's free, did he decide to put Krane's daughter on ice?

David LeGrand—The master telepath has offered his help in the investigation, but is it a setup to boost his fame?

COMPLICATIONS: David LeGrand has touched Nancy's heart. The problem is, he may only be playing with her mind.

Books in The Nancy Drew Files® Series

Available from ARCHWAY Paperbacks

The Nancy Drew Files™

116

UNDER HIS SPELL

CAROLYN KEENE

AN ARCHWAY PAPERBACK
Published by POCKET BOOKS
New York London Toronto Sydney Tokyo Singapore

AN ARCHWAY PAPERBACK *Original*

 An Archway Paperback published by
POCKET BOOKS, a division of Simon & Schuster Inc.
1230 Avenue of the Americas, New York, NY 10020

Copyright © 1996 by Simon & Schuster Inc.
Produced by Mega-Books, Inc.

ISBN: 0-671-50372-3

First Archway Paperback printing August 1996

10 9 8 7 6 5 4 3 2 1

NANCY DREW, AN ARCHWAY PAPERBACK and colophon are registered trademarks of Simon & Schuster Inc.

THE NANCY DREW FILES is a trademark of Simon & Schuster Inc.

Cover photograph from "Nancy Drew" Series © 1995 Nelvana Limited/Marathon Productions S.A. All rights reserved.

Logo design TM & © 1995 by Nelvana Limited. All rights reserved.

Printed in the U.S.A.

IL 6+

UNDER HIS SPELL

Chapter

One

"GREAT PARTY, huh, Nancy?" Bess Marvin's blue eyes twinkled as she moved to the loud, pulsing beat of the music. She shook her blond hair off her pretty face and smiled. "I knew it would be—Madame Tatiana predicted it."

Bess's friend Nancy Drew rolled her eyes. "Come on, Bess," she said. "You don't really believe all that psychic stuff, do you?"

"Of course I do," Bess said. "You would, too, if you'd let me take you to meet Madame Tatiana. She's different from all those phony psychics, Nan—she's for real."

"I'm sure." Nancy laughed and shook her head. Maybe it was because of the extrasensory convention that was being held in River Heights that weekend, but the occult had become Bess's passion of the moment. Personally, Nancy found

1

psychics pretty hard to take seriously, but by now she was used to her friend's sudden enthusiasms.

"Come on, Bess, let's party," Nancy said, changing the subject. "This DJ is awesome!"

It was Friday night, and Nancy and Bess had both been looking forward to this party all week. Morgan Shepherd, a former classmate of theirs, was hosting it. Her family was one of the wealthiest in River Heights, and Morgan's parties were famous.

Already the huge living room was packed with dancers, while rented laser lights played over the walls, and top-quality speakers boomed out the hits the hired DJ played one after the other.

"It doesn't take a psychic to guess that this party is going to be hot," Nancy commented as she and Bess threaded their way through the mob of dancers toward the refreshments table. "It's too bad George can't be here."

George Fayne, Bess's cousin and Nancy's close friend, was away in Colorado for a few days of skiing.

"Mmm-hmm," Bess said, not really paying attention. She kept looking around the room. "Madame said I'd be meeting the man of my dreams soon. I wonder if he's here. . . ."

Nancy was about to make another skeptical remark, but she bit her tongue. If Bess wanted to enjoy a little romantic speculation, who was

Nancy to get in the way? Besides, Bess was always falling in love, so Madame's prediction was probably a safe one.

"What does the man of your dreams look like?" Nancy asked as she got in line behind several other people who were waiting for soft drinks to be served.

"Oh, he's got dark hair and blue eyes," Bess said dreamily. "And big, big muscles . . ."

"Like Tommy Rio, for instance?" Nancy asked.

"Tommy Rio?" Bess repeated, surprised. "No way, Nan. He's going with Sharon Krane. Where have you been? They've been together forever."

"Oh, yeah?" Nancy asked. "That's what I thought, too. But there he is, dancing with Morgan. And don't look now, but he keeps checking *you* out every few seconds."

"What?" Bess started to turn and look but stopped herself. "Are you sure, Nan? I can't believe it! Where's Sharon? Do you see her anywhere?"

Nancy looked around, trying to spot Sharon Krane's slim figure and long, curly, dark hair. She'd know Sharon anywhere, though it had been years since they'd really spent much time together. Actually, Nancy knew Sharon's father better. He was a captain with the River Heights Police Department, and Nancy had worked with him on several cases.

3

Now she saw Sharon, dancing with a blond-haired guy Nancy didn't recognize. Sharon was wearing a short flippy skirt, a white T-shirt, and a blue denim jacket with sequins embroidered on both lapels. She wore the jacket with the sleeves half rolled up. A pair of iridescent fan-shaped earrings dangled from her ears.

"There she is," Nancy said, pointing. "I don't know, Bess. Maybe Sharon and Tommy have broken up since we last saw them."

"Could be," Bess said, arching an eyebrow. "I think I'll just find out. See you later, Nan. Opportunity may be knocking."

Bess disappeared onto the dance floor as the lights dimmed and starlike projections rotated on the walls and ceiling. A slow dance number came on over the speakers, and the DJ announced, "Here's a tune in honor of the extra-sensory convention beginning tomorrow. Everybody out on the floor for Jet Lag and their megahit, 'Second Sight'!"

Nancy asked the waiter for some ginger ale. Once she was served, she turned and looked around again. She saw that Bess was now dancing with Tommy Rio. Bess's arms were around his shoulders, and she was gazing into his eyes. But Nancy noticed that every now and then Tommy would cast his glance in another direction—across the floor to where Sharon was dancing with the blond newcomer. And the look in Tommy's eyes was anything but romantic. Furious was more like it, Nancy thought.

Morgan Shepherd came up to greet her. "Nancy!" she cooed, giving Nancy a peck on the cheek. "I'm glad you could make it."

"Great party, Morgan," Nancy said with a smile. "Say, who's the guy dancing with Sharon Krane?"

"Oooh, isn't he special?" Morgan said. "His name's Rick Roberts, and his family just moved to town. I can't wait to get to know him better."

"Looks as if he and Sharon have already gotten to know each other pretty well," Nancy pointed out.

Morgan frowned. "It's the weirdest thing," she said. "Sharon and Tommy walked in together, but they haven't gone near each other for the past hour. I'm dying of curiosity. In fact, I think I'm going to cut in on Rick and Sharon. Maybe I'll find out. And if not, at least I'll get Rick's attention." With a quick wink at Nancy, Morgan headed off.

As Nancy was finishing her ginger ale, a tall, dark-haired guy asked her to dance. She loved dancing, and she was having such a good time that a whole hour went by before she thought to look for Bess. Nancy didn't see her out on the dance floor, so she began to wander through the many rooms of the ground floor of the mansion, where guests were mingling, talking, and eating.

Finally Nancy found herself standing by open French doors that led out onto the huge back porch. Outside, under the stars, couples were holding hands, kissing, whispering to each other, and looking up at the sky. Nancy wandered outside, breathing in the cool, fresh air, and thinking of Ned Nickerson, her longtime boyfriend, who was away at Emerson College. She missed him so much sometimes.

Nancy had gone out with other guys while Ned was away. She had even been attracted to a few. But it just wasn't the same as being with Ned. And on a starry night like this, with songs of love playing in the background and other couples sharing the moment, Ned's absence hit Nancy really hard.

As she wandered out into the gardens behind the house, she suddenly heard Tommy Rio's deep voice. Thinking Bess might be with him, Nancy made her way in that direction. But the answering voice wasn't Bess's—it was Sharon Krane's. And Sharon sounded angry. So did Tommy, for that matter.

"I see it didn't take you long," Tommy was saying.

"Look," Sharon said. "I said I'd come to the party with you. But that was all. We're both free agents now, so whoever I dance with is really none of your business."

"I'm making it my business." Tommy's voice took on a threatening note.

"It looked like you were having a good time without me, anyway," Sharon retorted.

"That's right, I was!" Tommy said. "And I don't see why I shouldn't."

"You should! That's just the point!" Sharon shot back.

Nancy backed away, not wanting to intrude on the couple's privacy. Obviously, Sharon and Tommy were in the middle of a serious fight. Nancy made her way back inside and thought no more about it, until half an hour later. That's when she saw Sharon storm through the main room and out the front door, her bag slung over her shoulder and tears in her eyes.

Ten minutes later Nancy saw Tommy Rio come looking for Sharon—or at least it appeared that way. Tommy seemed on the verge of an explosion as he asked Morgan something. Morgan pointed to the front door, and Tommy ran toward it.

Nancy wondered again what it was all about. But then, someone tapped her on the shoulder and asked her to dance. Nancy turned her thoughts to happier things.

"Hi, Nan!" Bess said as she marched into the Drews' kitchen late the following morning. "Got anything to eat?"

"I think I can find you something," Nancy said with a smile. Bess was always fighting to keep her cute figure, but she was never able to resist snacking for very long. "Hannah's away for the weekend, but she made a batch of muffins yesterday." Hannah Gruen was the Drews' longtime housekeeper.

"Yum," Bess said, then sat down at the table. "Look what I brought you." She took a deck of cards out of her bag and began shuffling them. "I'm going to tell you your future."

Nancy raised an eyebrow but didn't answer. She placed two muffins in front of Bess.

"Madame Tatiana says I have psychic talent," Bess confided as she took a bite of a muffin.

"Is that so?" Nancy asked.

"You have to see her for yourself, Nan. I mean, I can read your cards, but I'm just a beginner. Madame's incredible. The first time she read my cards, she knew everything about me!"

"Is she going to have a booth at the extrasensory convention?" Nancy asked.

"No," Bess said. "She doesn't like doing that kind of thing. But I can't believe they didn't ask her to perform at night. They only invited well-known psychics like David LeGrand."

"David LeGrand . . ." Nancy said slowly. "I've heard of him. He's the guy who solved those kidnapping cases for the Chicago police last year, isn't he?"

"That's him," Bess confirmed. "And, Nan, he's soooo cute! And he's performing tonight. Wait till you see him. *Then* you'll believe in the supernatural, all right."

"Wait a minute," Nancy interrupted her. "Did I say I was going?"

"No," Bess said with a sly grin. "But *I* said so." She pulled two tickets out of her bag. "For you and me, for tonight. My treat, Nan. And don't you dare say no—you're coming and that's that."

Nancy shook her head as she smiled back at her friend. "Looks like I don't have a choice," she said. "So you say he's cute?"

"You won't regret it," Bess assured her. "Wait till you see David LeGrand do his thing, Nan. You'll be a believer then. And if you're not, you're coming with me this week to Madame Tatiana's."

Nancy had to laugh, but before she could object to Bess's plans, the telephone rang. To Nancy's surprise, it was Captain Philip Krane on the line.

"Nancy," he said, his voice sounding more upset than she had ever heard it before, "I need you to come down to headquarters right away. It's an emergency."

"Sure, Captain," Nancy said. "Can you tell me what it's about?"

"It's about Sharon," he said. "I understand you were at the same party she was last night?"

"Yes," Nancy said, concerned. "Is Sharon all right?"

"I hope so," Captain Krane said, his voice catching. "Sharon left that party, but she never came home. And no one has seen her since!"

Chapter

Two

NANCY TOLD Captain Krane she was on her way, then hung up and quickly explained to Bess what was going on.

"Oh, Nan! Do you think Sharon's okay? I mean, what if something terrible happened?"

"I'm worried, too," Nancy said as she grabbed her shoulder bag and car keys.

"Should I come with you?" Bess asked.

Nancy thought for a moment. "The best thing you can do right now is to call around to anyone we know who was at the party that night. Maybe one of them saw or heard something they forgot to tell the police."

Nancy handed Bess the phone book. "I'll call you when I know more." Without waiting for an answer, Nancy headed out the door and jumped into her blue Mustang convertible.

She drove straight to police headquarters. After parking in front of the building, she hurried inside. Nancy had been there on many cases, but she had never seen the place like this. A grim silence seemed to drape the entire headquarters. Even her old friend Chief McGinnis couldn't manage a smile in greeting her.

She was shown into Captain Krane's office. The captain sat behind his desk, his head in his hands. He looked up at Nancy and smiled wanly. "Hello, Nancy. It's good to see you again."

"I wish it were on happier business," Nancy said, taking a seat opposite him. "Okay, I'm ready. Tell me everything."

The captain sighed and began. "Sharon never came home last night. Early this morning, when I realized she wasn't in her room, I started calling around. Nothing. I called Tommy Rio—her boyfriend. He told me they'd had a little spat, and Sharon had left the party without him. So I got a list of people who attended the party, and several other people verified Tommy's story."

He got up and began pacing the room, now and then running a hand through his thinning gray hair. "I don't mind telling you, Nancy, I'm really worried. It's not like Sharon to go off this way."

"I take it you don't think she ran away on her own," Nancy said.

Krane shook his head. "It would be totally out

of character. But on the other hand, there's been no ransom note and no phone calls. One passerby has her walking down Danbury Road, half a mile from the Shepherd house, heading toward town at around midnight. That jibes with Tommy's version. He said she left the party around eleven forty-five."

The captain sat down again and began drumming his fingers on the desk. "My people have searched every inch of ground between that spot on the road and town. Nothing. Not a trace of her. There were a lot of people at the party, and we haven't had time to question them all yet. But so far nobody's had anything new to tell us."

"So you decided to call me in," Nancy said.

"Well, you were there, too," Krane said. "And you know Sharon."

"Sort of," Nancy hedged. "We haven't seen much of each other lately." Sharon could have changed a lot since the days when the two of them had hung out together.

"Anyway, you've been such a help to the department in the past, I thought you might be willing—"

"Of course," Nancy said. "Anything I can do."

"The worst part of it is," Krane said, leaning forward, "Sharon's a diabetic."

"You're kidding!" Nancy drew in a sharp breath. "I had no idea."

"She was diagnosed a year ago," Krane told

13

her. "She needs injections every day. If some-one's holding her, she could be in real trouble. She needs her insulin to survive, Nancy. She carries a couple of vials of insulin with her at all times, but those would only get her through forty-eight hours. After that . . ."

He didn't need to say anything else. Nancy counted back to the party. By Sunday night at the latest Sharon would be running out of medi-cine.

"Any suspects?" Nancy asked. "I mean, going on the theory she was kidnapped." She didn't need to mention the horrible alternative—that they might already be too late to save Sharon.

"Well, there's Tommy Rio," Krane began. "He and Sharon have been having problems, and he admitted that they had words at the party."

"Did he say what the fight was about?" Nancy asked, recalling the bits of conversation she'd overheard in the garden.

"He said it was about his wanting to date other girls," Krane told her.

Nancy frowned. That's not how it had sounded to her. "Did Sharon ever talk with you about her relationship with Tommy?" she asked.

Krane sighed and shook his head. "Only in the beginning, when things were going well. Sharon's not . . . since her mother died . . . You see, it was always her mom Sharon confided in when she had problems. I guess I'm not an easy guy to talk to. . . ."

"Don't blame yourself," Nancy said quickly. "It's hard for a lot of teens to open up to their parents. But we both know Sharon loves you—and she needs you now, more than ever before."

"You're right, of course," the captain said. "Thanks, Nancy. I guess I needed to hear that." He blew out a long breath. "Anyway, there's Tommy. He says he didn't leave with Sharon, but one person said she saw Tommy leave not long afterward."

"I can verify that," Nancy said, nodding. "It couldn't have been more than ten minutes later."

"So he could have followed her in his car. She was walking, remember." Captain Krane frowned and shook his head. "She must have been pretty upset, to be walking all the way home. I mean, it's only a couple of miles, but she knows better than to walk alone at night. If only she'd called me . . ."

"Any other suspects?" Nancy asked gently.

Krane hesitated for a moment. "There *is* one other person. His name is Eddie Hill. He's an ex-convict, a guy I helped send to prison for a long time. He was released just last month. And I know from friends of mine in corrections that Eddie's been swearing revenge on me and my whole family since the day of his armed robbery conviction."

"Sounds bad," Nancy said.

Krane nodded grimly. "I've already hauled him in for questioning, and he didn't have a very good alibi for last night—home alone, watching TV, he said. Still, we searched both his and Tommy Rio's houses and cars—nothing. And I've got to find Sharon quickly, Nancy. Her life may depend on it."

"Count me in," Nancy said. "I'll start by speaking to Tommy Rio and Eddie Hill myself, if that's okay with you. Something might come out that the police missed. No offense, but you know how criminals get their guard up when they see a uniform."

"Sure," the captain agreed. He was busy writing down addresses for Nancy. "Here," he said, handing them to her. "Good luck. And call me as soon as you're done."

"Of course," Nancy said. "By the way, have you contacted the media? If you make it known Sharon's missing, somebody might spot her."

Krane nodded. "There's a reporter from *Today's Times* on her way here right now. I'm giving her a statement to include in Sunday's edition. I'm offering amnesty, no questions asked, for Sharon's return. Also, if Sharon's not back tomorrow, I'm taping a TV appeal. I need to alert whoever's got her that she must have insulin. Soon Sharon may not be able to speak for herself. . . ." he finished, his voice trailing off.

Nancy gave him a sympathetic look, then left. On the steps of the building, she nearly ran into a well-dressed young woman.

"Nancy Drew!" she said. "Well, what a surprise to see you here."

"Hello, Brenda," Nancy said, managing a weak smile. Brenda Carlton, a reporter for *Today's Times,* was forever nosing her way into Nancy's cases, interfering and ruining everything in her pursuit of a juicy story.

"So, this must be really big, huh?" Brenda asked, whipping out her notepad and pen. "They've got you in on it already. Okay, Drew—dish."

"No way, Brenda," Nancy told her. "You can get all you need from Captain Krane."

"Is that so?" Brenda asked, arching an eyebrow. "Something tells me I'll be seeing more of you before too long, Drew."

"Tell me, Brenda," Nancy said dryly, "since when does the *Times* send their gossip columnist to cover the police beat?" Before Brenda could say a word, Nancy turned and ran down the steps to her car.

Tommy Rio answered the door of his family's modest two-story house. He seemed surprised to see Nancy, but then he gave her a look of grim understanding. "Hi, Nancy," he said. "Or should I say 'Detective Drew'?"

"This is serious, Tommy," Nancy said. "Sharon may be in real trouble."

"Sorry," he said, brushing his dark hair off his forehead and stepping back from the door so that Nancy could enter.

She stepped into the simply furnished living room and sat in an armchair. Tommy lowered his big, athletic frame onto a sofa opposite her.

"How'd you know about me being a detective?" Nancy asked.

"Sharon once mentioned that you were working on a case with her father. I guess the police called you in, huh?" he asked, eyeing her carefully. "Look, I already told them everything I know."

"Let's just go over it again, okay?" Nancy said. "How long had you and Sharon been going out?"

"Oh, seven or eight months," Tommy said. "We were pretty serious about each other, if that's what you're getting at."

"But she didn't leave the party with you," Nancy prodded.

"Uh, yeah," Tommy said, shifting uncomfortably on the sofa. "We had kind of a fight," he admitted. "I offered to drive her home when she insisted on leaving, but she wouldn't let me. She said she'd rather walk. But I didn't believe she'd really do it." He shrugged. "I guess she was pretty steamed at me."

"What about?" Nancy asked.

There was a slight, almost undetectable pause before he answered. "I'd started seeing other girls. Sharon didn't like that. When she saw me dancing with Morgan Shepherd, it really set her off, you know?"

Nancy sat quietly, looking at him, trying to make Tommy's story fit with what she'd seen and heard at the party. There was no way.

"Tommy," she said, "I was there. I saw Sharon dancing with that new guy in town. She didn't even seem to notice you and Morgan."

Was she imagining it, or did Tommy's face redden when she said that?

"I guess she had you fooled, too," Tommy said with a forced chuckle. "I thought she didn't mind, until later, when she dragged me outside and started laying into me about it."

Nancy thought back to the conversation she'd overheard. There was no mistaking the meaning of Sharon's words.

"You know what, Tommy?" Nancy said, leaning forward. "I think you're not being straight with me. I think it was Sharon who wanted to start seeing other people, and you who wanted to stop her."

Tommy tried to laugh off Nancy's words, but

the smile froze on his face. "You don't know what you're talking about," he snarled.

"Oh, yes, I do," Nancy said, getting up. "If you know anything about where Sharon is, Tommy, I'd advise you to come clean about it—now. You see, I happened to overhear the two of you arguing. And if I were you, I'd call Captain Krane right now and tell him the truth. Because if you don't, I will."

"Are you threatening me?" Tommy asked, rising to his feet.

"Only if you're not telling the truth," she said levelly. "Are you threatening *me?*"

Tommy glared down at her, on the brink of explosion. Then, with an effort, he seemed to pull himself together. "Don't be ridiculous. Why should I care what you do? I have nothing to hide."

"I hope that's true," Nancy said quietly. And with that, she made her way to the door, leaving Tommy Rio staring after her.

Nancy took a deep breath as she stepped outside and strode toward her car. If Tommy was jealous of Sharon's going out with other guys, and hot enough to deny it, Nancy thought, maybe he was angry enough to harm Sharon after all. Nancy hoped not.

Nancy had to check her map to find the address Captain Krane had given her for Eddie

Hill, ex-convict. It was in a run-down area on the outskirts of town.

Nancy pulled up in front of a small, dilapidated house and got out of her car. She walked up the sagging wooden steps and knocked on the front door. Her knock was answered by a tall man with blond hair cropped short. He had the chest and arms of a bodybuilder and a sneering look on his face. "Yeah?" he said. "What are you selling? I ain't buying nothing, okay?"

"Eddie Hill?" Nancy asked, holding her ground.

"Yeah, that's me," he said, looking her over with cold, penetrating blue eyes. "What do you want?"

"I'm a friend of Sharon Krane's," Nancy said. "I was wondering if you might know where she is."

"Krane!" Nancy saw the hatred in Eddie's eyes. "Who sent you?" he asked menacingly. "Who?" He reached out and grabbed Nancy's arm.

"If you don't know where Sharon is, maybe you wouldn't mind me checking inside, just to prove she's not here," Nancy suggested boldly.

"Listen," Eddie almost spat, his face only inches from hers. "You get out of my life, and stay out—or I'll do a lot worse to you than's been done to Sharon Krane."

Chapter

Three

NANCY SLOWLY FREED HERSELF from Eddie's grip and backed away. "Okay," she said, keeping her voice steady. "I'm going."

"Good idea." Eddie went back inside and slammed the door. Nancy didn't hang around. She'd been threatened, but it wasn't herself she was worried about—it was Sharon Krane.

Would whoever had taken her realize she needed insulin? And how would they get it for her? For that matter, was Sharon even still alive?

When Nancy got home, Bess was no longer there. She'd left a note on the kitchen table, saying "Spoke to a bunch of people, but nobody knew anything. Call me and let me know what's happening." Nancy picked up the phone, dialed Bess's number, and told her the whole story.

"Oh, Nan!" Bess gasped when Nancy had

finished. "Do you think it was Eddie Hill? Or Tommy? I can't believe he'd hurt Sharon, can you?"

"I don't know, Bess," Nancy admitted. "Listen, at this point it's probably better if we don't say anything more about this to anybody, okay? Brenda Carlton's covering the story for the *Times*. We don't want to let out any details Captain Krane didn't tell Brenda about."

"Sure," Bess promised. "So—what about the show tonight? Are you still coming with me?"

Nancy blinked. "To tell you the truth, I'd forgotten all about it," she said.

"Nan, you have to come! David LeGrand has solved millions of kidnapping cases before. He can probably help find Sharon."

Nancy sighed. There was no arguing with Bess. "Why not?" she said. "At this point, I'll take any help I can get."

"Great!" Bess said. "I'll pick you up around seven. And I promise, you won't be disappointed."

The convention center was packed and buzzing with excitement when Nancy and Bess walked inside. "You won't regret this, Nan," Bess assured her.

There were some peculiar-looking people in the crowd milling around the lobby—women with turbans, men with capes. But strangest of all

23

was the woman Bess now dragged Nancy over to meet.

She looked like a caricature of a fortune-teller. Her flowing ankle-length dress was a deep purple, and a big red jewel hung around her neck. She wore rings on every finger, hoop earrings, and numerous bracelets.

"Nancy," Bess said proudly, "meet Madame Tatiana Dove. Madame, this is Nancy. You remember I told you about her?"

"Ah, yes. Nancy . . . Drew, isn't it? I feel as if I know you already."

"Amazing," Nancy said, stifling a grin. Luckily, the lights began flashing on and off, signaling that the show was about to begin. Nancy was spared having her mind read, at least for the moment.

Madame's seat was up front, unlike those Bess had managed to get for herself and Nancy. So the three parted company. "Isn't she fantastic?" Bess asked Nancy.

"That's a good word for her," Nancy agreed. Just before they entered the auditorium, Nancy spotted a poster of a dark, magnetically handsome young man in his twenties with deep-set eyes and a haunting gaze. Underneath the picture were the words "David LeGrand, master clairvoyant."

"That's him, huh?" Nancy asked Bess.

"Uh-huh. Isn't he gorgeous?"

Nancy nodded. If David LeGrand was as talented as he was good-looking, they were in for a treat.

They took their seats just as the lights went down. A spotlight came on and followed David LeGrand as he walked onstage, dressed in a black tuxedo. The crowd welcomed him enthusiastically. The psychic nodded and held up his hand to stop the applause.

"Ladies and gentlemen," he began, "thank you for your warm welcome. It's very generous of you, since I haven't done anything yet." He smiled, then went on. "Now, I know some of you may not be believers. I'm not asking you to be. All I'm asking is that you watch—and draw your own conclusions."

And with that, David LeGrand proceeded to put on the most astonishing demonstration of psychic skills Nancy had ever seen. He picked strangers out of the audience and told them the contents of their pockets, their handbags, their wallets. He had people whisper things to their neighbors and then told them what they'd said. He had people write things down on paper and throw them into a hat, then picked them out at random and, without unfolding the papers, read them and guessed who had written them.

Each trick—if they were tricks, and even Nancy wasn't sure—was more baffling than the last. The psychic had an open, simple approach.

25

He was totally unlike what Nancy had expected from a famous clairvoyant.

When the performance was over, he stepped to the front of the stage and once again held up his hands for silence. "Ladies and gentlemen," he said, "I regret to inform you that this will be my last performance of the weekend."

A murmur ran through the audience. "I'm sorry to disappoint those of you who may have wanted to recommend the show to your friends. But it seems that my services are needed for something more important. I have been called in to help the River Heights Police Department on a most urgent matter. I'm not at liberty to tell you about it since it hasn't appeared in the media yet. I hope you'll understand."

He took a final bow, to thunderous applause, and left the stage. Nancy looked at Bess. "Are you thinking what I'm thinking?" Bess asked her.

"It's got to be the Sharon Krane case," Nancy agreed. "Come on. Let's go backstage and see!"

An usher pointed them toward the backstage area. There, they encountered an older woman wearing a pin that read Staff. She was standing outside a partially open dressing room door. "No visitors!" she said curtly. "Convention center policy."

Then a voice behind her said, "Somebody to see me? Let them in, I've changed already."

The older woman frowned but stepped aside so Nancy and Bess could enter.

There was David LeGrand, looking into Nancy's eyes. She couldn't help noticing he was even better-looking up close. His gaze was positively hypnotic.

"I'm Nancy Drew," she said, holding out her hand. "This is my friend Bess Marvin. We just saw your show. You were . . . incredible."

"Incredible!" Bess repeated.

David LeGrand smiled warmly. "Glad you liked it," he said. "Would you like me to sign your programs?"

"Oh, would you?" Bess cried.

The psychic's smile broadened into a grin, and he picked up a pen from his makeup table. As he was signing the programs, Nancy said, "Actually, I was interested in what you said at the end of the performance. It wouldn't be the Sharon Krane case you're working on, would it?"

David LeGrand stopped in midsignature and looked up at her, his eyes twinkling. "You must be psychic yourself," he said. "How did you know?"

"I'm working on the case," Nancy explained. "I'm a private detective, and Captain Krane called me in and asked me to help."

David LeGrand nodded. "From what I understand, he needs all the help he can get. People rarely call me in unless they're desperate. I'm afraid there isn't a lot of respect out there for what I do, in spite of my record."

Nancy didn't know what to say. Despite her skepticism about psychics, she felt strangely at ease with David LeGrand. His sincere manner and quiet confidence were so different from what she'd expected. And then there were those gorgeous eyes.

When the famous psychic handed them the signed programs, Bess said, "Thanks so much. Well, I guess you two want to talk about the case. Nan, I'll meet you in the lobby, okay?"

"Listen," the psychic said. "I'm supposed to go see Captain Krane right now. Do you want to go with me, Nancy?"

"Definitely!" Nancy said. "I'm interested to see how you work, Mr. LeGrand."

"Please—call me David," he said. "And I can drive you home afterward, if that's all right."

"Fine. David, then," Nancy said, embarrassed to feel herself blushing. "Bess . . . see you in the morning?"

"First thing!" Bess wiggled her eyebrows wickedly. "Have a nice night, Drew! 'Bye, David . . ." With a sigh Bess clutched the program to her chest and left the room.

David grabbed a garment bag. "Come on, then," he said. "We can go out the alley door instead of the stage door. I don't want to spend the next hour signing autographs. This girl's life may be hanging in the balance."

Nancy followed him out into the alleyway. "I've never been to River Heights," David said. "It's a nice town. Quite a contrast to Chicago. I just got through working there last night. You get tired of big cities after a while."

Just then Nancy heard a noise from behind some large trash cans that lined the alleyway. Something was back there. Probably a cat, Nancy guessed. Still, it made her uneasy.

Twice as they walked toward the street, Nancy thought she heard footsteps and turned around, only to find the alleyway still deserted.

They reached the street, and suddenly someone shouted, "There he is!"

In an instant they were besieged by a crowd of people, all clamoring for LeGrand's autograph. He gave Nancy a helpless shrug and said, "I'll just be a minute."

Nancy could tell it would be a bit longer than that, and she wanted to check out the alley, just to make sure no one was there. "I'll be right back," she told him, and threaded her way through the crowd.

The alley was silent and empty. Nancy stood there for a long moment, then decided she'd been mistaken.

It was as she turned away that something

moving caught her eye. Turning back, she saw a shadowy, masked figure, dressed in black, ducking behind a Dumpster at the far end of the alley. Someone had been following them after all!

Chapter

Four

NANCY DIDN'T HESITATE. The alley ran between two streets, and she raced to the end where it led onto busy Ridge Road. She looked around in all directions. Traffic was heavy for this time of night, and there were a lot of people on the street, many on their way home from the convention center.

The masked figure in black had disappeared. What had he been doing in that alley? Nancy wondered. Was he waiting there to rob someone? Or had he been following David LeGrand?

She turned and walked back down the alley, her eyes scanning the ground for anything in the way of a clue to the dark figure's identity. She found nothing and walked back to the crowd that still surrounded David LeGrand. He was signing autographs, with a helpless look on his face.

When he saw Nancy, he smiled gratefully and beckoned for her to follow him. He apologized to the rest of the disappointed crowd and led her to his rented car. He unlocked the door on Nancy's side. As she got in, David said, "I thought you'd deserted me there for a minute. Where did you go?"

"Someone was following us," Nancy said, looking up at him.

"Following us—who?" LeGrand exclaimed. "Did you get a good look at him?" He paused. "It was a him, wasn't it?"

"I'm pretty sure it was," Nancy said. "He looked big and muscular. And he's definitely athletic."

David looked over at the crowd of people, who were moving toward the car. "We'd better get going," he said.

As he started the car, David said, "I have a feeling you're a great detective." He smiled as he looked into her eyes. "Not to mention a beautiful one."

Nancy felt herself blushing. "You're very good at what you do, too," she said. "I admired your act."

David's smile widened as he pulled out of the parking space. "Thanks," he said. "But it's not an act. I'm not faking any of it, though a lot of people can't seem to believe that. Tell me,

Nancy. Do you believe in ESP—extrasensory perception?"

Nancy bit her lip. She didn't want to offend him, but she didn't want to lie to him, either. "I'm trying to keep an open mind," she told him. "You certainly opened my eyes tonight."

"And you, mine," he countered.

A few minutes later they reached the police station. David pulled into the restricted parking lot and explained to the duty officer who he was. Then he and Nancy went inside, straight to Captain Krane's office.

The captain clearly hadn't gotten any rest since she had seen him, Nancy thought. He looked awful. And she knew that his ordeal was probably far from over.

"Nancy!" Captain Krane said, getting up from his chair and coming over to them. "Hello, Mr. LeGrand," he said, shaking his hand. "I'm so glad you could come. Say, have you two already met?"

"Briefly," Nancy said. "I was at David's show tonight, and when he announced he was going to be working with the River Heights Police, I put two and two together and went backstage to meet him."

"I'm glad you did," David said. "I have the powerful sense that you are exceptional at what you do. I think we'll make a great team."

Nancy looked down at her shoes. She couldn't help feeling uncomfortable about the idea of being paired with a psychic—even an incredibly cute one.

The captain's eyes widened hopefully. "That's kind of what I was hoping for," he said. "Come in and sit down, both of you. I want to run down the details of the case for Mr. LeGrand, Nancy, and then you can tell me what you've been up to."

As Captain Krane went through the case, David listened carefully. Nancy couldn't help but be impressed again by his calm manner. Only once, when Captain Krane mentioned that Sharon was a diabetic, did the psychic become visibly upset. "But that's awful!" he said. "She could die if we don't find her soon!"

Then, seeming to realize he'd jolted the captain's fatherly feelings, David fell silent for the rest of Captain Krane's story.

Half an hour later the meeting was over. "You two can work together or separately, as you like," the captain told Nancy and LeGrand as they all stood. "But remember, time is everything. We can't waste a moment."

"I understand," David assured him. "And I'm sure Nancy doesn't need to be reminded. We'll report back to you as soon as we've found out anything."

Outside, David turned to Nancy and said, "Do

you need to get straight home? It's only eleven-thirty."

Nancy hesitated. She did want to get to know David LeGrand better. And she was surprised to find that the thought of working with him was starting to appeal to her. But she wasn't sure how his way of doing things and hers would mix.

"You're wondering how we can ever work together," he said suddenly. "You, so rational, so logical . . . me, so intuitive, so—well, I'm the furthest thing from scientific in the conventional sense, aren't I?"

Nancy smiled. "Hmmm, you really are psychic."

"This time I didn't have to read your mind." He laughed. "It was written all over your face. So, how about a cup of hot chocolate? I passed a café near my hotel. And I'm still good for that lift home afterward."

"Okay," Nancy said, relenting.

Ten minutes later they were sitting at a corner table in the café, and although the place was crowded, it seemed to Nancy that when David looked at her, there was a shield of privacy hiding the two of them from the rest of the world.

"Honestly," David said, peering at her over the top of his steaming mug, "what do you really think of paranormal phenomena?"

Nancy looked down. How could she put it so

35

that he wouldn't be offended? "I think what we call the supernatural is just things we can't understand yet. I'm the type who doesn't trust what can't be proved. I guess it's because my dad's a lawyer, and that's how he taught me to look at things."

David nodded and grinned at her. "I learned at home, too," he said. "My parents never told me anything, so I always had to guess what they were thinking."

Nancy laughed. "I know what you mean," she said. "David, what do you think really happened to Sharon Krane? I mean, they've searched Eddie Hill's house and Tommy Rio's, they've searched the road she was walking along—and they've found nothing. There's been no ransom note, no phone calls demanding money—"

"You want to know if I think she's dead," he responded quietly. Nancy returned his gaze. It was exactly what she wanted to know.

"I thought you didn't believe in guesswork," he reminded her.

"With most people, I don't," she replied. "In your case, however, I'm keeping an open mind."

"Fair enough," he said. "In that case I'd have to say Sharon Krane is definitely alive. For the moment. She's not far away, either."

"And what makes you so sure?" Nancy asked.

He thought for a moment, then said, "I really couldn't tell you. Impressions come into my mind. Strong impressions. I don't know where they come from, and I don't really care to know. All I care about is that they're almost always right. I trust my inner voices, Nancy. I think that's the difference between most people and me. Anyone could do what I do if they listened the right way. I really believe that."

"Okay," Nancy said. "So let's just say, for the moment, that Sharon's alive and nearby. How do we go about finding her?"

"Well, how do *you* do it?" David asked her.

Nancy was thoughtful for a moment. Then she said, "I look at the people who have motive and opportunity, and I check them out. For instance, I'd like to get inside Eddie Hill's house to have a look around. I know the police have already been through the place, but I might notice different things than they would."

"You're right," David said. "What else?"

"I want to find out more about Sharon and Tommy Rio's relationship."

"Sounds like a good idea," David agreed. "Me, I'm going to go back to my hotel room and get a good night's sleep. Some of my best information comes to me in my dreams. I'm positive that when I wake up tomorrow morning, I'll know how to proceed."

He paid the check, then drove her home and walked her to her door. "Get some sleep yourself," he told her. "Why don't you call me at the

Parkchester tomorrow morning, and I'll tell you what I'm up to, okay?"

"Okay," she answered.

His dark eyes seemed to see right through her. "I look forward to working with you, Nancy," he said in a near whisper. He gave her hand a gentle squeeze, then turned and headed back to his car.

Nancy went inside and got ready for bed. She lay there in the darkness for close to an hour, thinking about everything that had happened. She had just fallen asleep when she was jarred awake by the ringing of the telephone. The alarm clock by her bed told her it was two in the morning. This could only be trouble, she thought as she grabbed the receiver.

"Hello?" she said fuzzily.

"Nancy? It's Phil Krane." The police captain's voice had a trembling quality to it.

Nancy sat upright in bed. "What is it, Captain?" she asked, her heart pounding with dread.

"I just got home," he said, "and found a ransom note shoved under my door. They've got Sharon, Nancy—they've got my little girl!"

Chapter

Five

NANCY TOLD Captain Krane she'd be right over. Then she hung up, threw on a pair of jeans and a white, man's-style shirt, ran a comb through her shoulder-length reddish blond hair, and hurried downstairs. After scribbling a note for her father, she raced for her car. In less than fifteen minutes she was at the Krane house. But as she drove up and parked at the curb, she noticed that someone else had already beaten her there. David LeGrand's rental car was parked in Krane's driveway.

Nancy was surprised to feel a tiny twinge of jealousy. She had helped the River Heights Police Department solve a number of cases, and here they were calling in a psychic.

True, David LeGrand had found kidnapping victims before. But Nancy was still not con-

vinced that he had some kind of magical power.
She still believed "extrasensory perception" just
meant someone was good at picking up subtle
clues.

She rang the doorbell and waited. It was soon
answered by Captain Krane, who looked even
worse than he had earlier at the station. Over his
shoulder Nancy saw David LeGrand, holding a
plastic bag with what looked like a letter inside.

"Come on in, Nancy," the captain said, making way for her. "And thanks."

"No thanks required," Nancy told him. "Hello, David."

"Hi, Nancy," he said. "We have to stop meeting like this."

She flashed him a brief smile. "Is that the
note?" she asked.

He handed her the transparent bag, and she
read the note. It was hand-printed in pencil in a
terribly awkward handwriting. "Almost as if
someone wrote it with the wrong hand," Nancy
commented.

The note read:

WE HAVE SHARON. WE WANT $250,000
BY TOMORROW MIDNIGHT OR SHE
DIES. DROP IN RIVERSIDE PARK BY OLD
OAK TREE NEAR BOATHOUSE. PUT
MONEY IN CLEAR PLASTIC BAG. DON'T
TRY ANYTHING FOOLISH.

Nancy looked up to find Captain Krane staring expectantly at her. "What do you make of it?" he asked.

"This was done by a righty writing lefty or vice versa," Nancy said. "Otherwise, it's pretty straightforward. This person's careful. Riverside Park's a clever drop point because it's so narrow and there's a steep slope down from the road to the river. From a car or a boat the kidnapper can see if anyone's there, make a quick pickup and escape. Midnight Sunday night's a good time, too. Not many people in the park, but not deserted, either. The kidnapper will be able to sneak up on the money and check things out," she continued, "without making himself obvious as the criminal." Nancy walked the room, ransom note in hand, thinking.

"This may even be a test run," she concluded, "to see if you really drop the money or if the area will be surrounded by police. And of course, to make us even more desperate."

"He's playing with Sharon's life doing that!" the captain said in a hoarse voice.

"He's been playing with it from the very beginning," Nancy reminded him. "This is not the sort of person who cares about other people's feelings."

Nancy stopped pacing. "How are you going to get that much money together?" she asked softly.

"I can't get that kind of money together," he said. "I'm not a rich man, Nancy."

The truth of it suddenly hit her. The Kranes lived in a modest, three-bedroom house. Captain Krane earned a decent salary, but they certainly weren't rich. "Why you, then?" she asked. "Why Sharon? There's something strange about all this."

"My thoughts exactly," the captain said. "What do you think, LeGrand? Any suggestions?"

"I'd like to see the note again," he said.

Nancy handed it to him. He closed his eyes and held it close to his face, seeming to breathe it in. "I'll need a few minutes to concentrate, to get a sense of Sharon's presence. The letter's been near her, I can tell that already. It will help me to track her."

"Do you want to be alone?" the captain asked him.

"Just for a few minutes," the psychic answered, still with his eyes closed.

Captain Krane motioned to Nancy, and they went into the dining room together. "Well?" he asked when they were out of earshot. "What do you think? Is this guy for real?"

Nancy shrugged. "He's very good at what he does—whatever that is. I saw his show."

"I'm still a little skeptical," Krane confessed. "But I guess that's just the way I'm built. Everyone says LeGrand's the best. He solved two kidnappings in Chicago. Me, I never thought I'd be calling in a psychic on a kidnapping case." He sighed. "But it's my own daughter this time. Now I really know how those parents feel whose kids are missing. I'll try anything."

"Even giving the kidnappers a quarter of a million dollars?" Nancy asked.

"If I could, I would," he confessed. "I wasn't going to say anything yet—I don't want to get my hopes up. But Chief McGinnis is calling in the FBI, and they may be able to work out something, but they can't get it together in twenty-four hours. So I'm going to do exactly what you said the kidnapper is doing. I'm going to make this a trial run. I'm going to get a SWAT detail lined up, throw a dragnet around the park and roadblocks around the whole town. Plainclothes, counterfeit money, unmarked vehicles. If this guy's an amateur, we'll get him. If he's a pro, he won't hurt Sharon. He'll just up the price."

"And if he's a guy with a personal grudge?" Nancy asked, thinking of Eddie Hill.

Krane frowned. "I've got a tail on Eddie and on Tommy Rio, too. If they make a move, I'll be down on them so fast they won't know what hit them."

Nancy nodded. It sounded like the best possible plan under the circumstances.

Just then David LeGrand appeared in the

doorway. "I've got an energy reading," he said. "But it's very faint. Can we go for a drive?"

"We'll take my car!" Krane exclaimed. As if he'd been starving for action, he grabbed his keys and his jacket, and strode quickly for the front door.

A few minutes later they were driving down the deserted streets of River Heights. David sat in the front seat, next to Captain Krane, who was driving at a steady twenty miles per hour. Nancy rode in the back.

They traveled eastward, nearly to the edge of town, on a meandering route. David's eyes were closed much of the time. Every now and then, he'd suddenly say, "Right at the corner" or "left at the light." Otherwise, all three were silent. Watching David, Nancy felt that strange tug inside her—skeptical on the one hand, attracted on the other.

"The vibrations are very strong here," David said suddenly as they passed a parking lot behind a row of warehouses. Captain Krane drove into the lot and killed the engine. They all stepped out of the car and stood there, listening.

The warehouses looked abandoned. In the distance a night freight train blew its whistle. Cars passed on a highway not far away, but there were no human sounds.

David started walking toward the rear of one

of the warehouses. Nancy and Krane followed him, darting occasional glances at each other.

In his hand the psychic held the ransom note. He stopped walking near the back entrance of the abandoned building. He blinked, then turned to face Captain Krane. "I don't know," he said, shaking his head in confusion. "I'm sure I picked up something."

"I'm going to have a look inside this place," Captain Krane said, gazing at the building. He used his car phone and called in reinforcements. Then he tested the building's windows until he found one that opened. "You stay out here," he told Nancy and David. "I'll just be a minute—I hope."

Nancy looked at her watch. If he wasn't back in three minutes, she'd go in after him, Nancy decided. But Captain Krane appeared at the window almost immediately, a frown on his face.

"Nobody's been in there for months," he announced as he climbed out the window. "Spiderwebs all over the place. Not even a footprint."

"I'm—I'm sorry," David said. "I'll try again if you like. I was so sure. . . ."

They all stood there silently. Nancy felt for David LeGrand. He seemed so crestfallen that his talents had come up short.

"Well," David said, "we may as well leave. I'm sorry to have dragged you out here, Captain."

"It's okay," the captain said with a sigh. He fished in his pocket for the car keys.

As they turned to go, Nancy's gaze swept the warehouses and parking lot, searching for anything they'd missed. Her ears were alert for unusual sounds.

Suddenly she noticed a lone Dumpster standing in weeds, away from the warehouse. Without a word she walked over to it, hoisted herself up, and shone her flashlight inside.

"I see something!" she shouted to the others. Reaching her arm downward, she pulled out a torn blue denim jacket with sequins embroidered on both lapels.

"It's Sharon's jacket!" Nancy exclaimed. "She was wearing it at the party Friday night!"

Chapter
Six

CAPTAIN KRANE WAS SHAKING with rage. "Whoever did this, I'll make them pay!" he rumbled, taking the torn jacket from Nancy and clutching it to his chest.

Then he turned to David. "I want to thank you, LeGrand," he said. "I've got to be honest with you. Up till this very moment I wouldn't have given you two cents for any psychic I'd ever met. But you're the real thing. If you can find my Sharon, I'll be eternally grateful."

"Nancy's the one you should be thanking," David said. "She went right for that Dumpster."

"Right," the captain mumbled, nodding.

Nancy felt a brief twinge at not being recognized for her contribution. But she refused to let it get to her. "Could I see the jacket for a moment, Captain?"

She took it from him and looked through all the pockets. They were empty. Then, just as she was about to hand the jacket back, she saw something—a piece of paper, tucked into the rolled-up sleeve.

She pulled it out and saw that it was a note, quickly dashed off in pencil, on lined paper.

"'Sharon,'" Nancy read out loud. "'I can't believe you're doing this. It can't end between us. I won't let it. If you don't get back together with me, I don't know what I'll do. Don't make it come to that. Please. Love forever, T.R.'"

The three of them stood in surprised silence. "The boy lied to me," Captain Krane finally said. "He told me he was the one who wanted to break it off."

"He told me the same thing," Nancy said. She'd already known Tommy was lying; it was the tone of Tommy's note that worried her. He sounded desperate. And while Nancy couldn't see what Tommy could hope to gain by kidnapping Sharon, there was another, far more horrible, possibility. What if Tommy had hurt or even killed Sharon—in a rage or accidentally—and had sent a phony ransom note to make the police think it was a kidnapping?

"Even if he did lie about things, it doesn't mean Tommy's guilty," Nancy pointed out to the captain, keeping her worries to herself for the moment. "It's possible that he has too much pride to admit Sharon would break up with him." She sighed. "But it sure does make him look like our number-one suspect."

"I'm going to get a warrant and search the kid's house again," Krane said. "I'm going to haul him in for questioning. I'm going to scare the living daylights out of him until he tells me where Sharon is!"

"I think that would be jumping the gun, Captain," David said gently. "We need to stay calm. You say you've had him under observation. You've searched his house already, and Sharon isn't there. So even if you question Tommy again, he may not confess, and you still don't have any real proof. Why not wait and see if he's the one who shows up at the drop-off point tonight?"

Captain Krane sighed. "You're right," he said. "I'm reacting emotionally because it's my daughter. I need to step back and be as objective as I would in any other case. And now, as soon as my people show up to search this place, I'll drive you two back."

Just then three squad cars pulled up, and a group of officers hurried over. Behind them a red sports car screeched to a stop, and Brenda Carlton hopped out.

"All right, what's going on?" she asked as soon as she reached Nancy. "And don't try ducking me, Nancy. It won't work. I know you're onto something."

Nancy shook her head in frustration and referred Brenda to Captain Krane. He gave the reporter a statement, mentioning everything but the note Nancy had found in the jacket's sleeve and the ransom note. Brenda's eyes widened like saucers. As Brenda held the microphone of her tape recorder up to the captain's face, Nancy saw the reporter look over at David LeGrand and heard her sigh.

"Psychic as hero," Nancy heard her whisper. "Great angle!" Running over to David, Brenda cooed, "Mr. LeGrand, in light of all that's happened, would you consent to being interviewed for the *Times?*"

The psychic closed his eyes briefly, then smiled graciously. "Of course," he said. "But not right now, please. I'm tired. If you'll call me at my hotel, the Parkchester, I'm sure we can arrange something."

"Of course," Brenda echoed, smiling at him flirtatiously. "I'm all yours. Whenever."

Give me a break, Nancy thought. Sometimes she really couldn't stand Brenda Carlton.

A short while later Captain Krane drove Nancy and David back to his house, where they said good night and got into their own cars. The captain promised to call Nancy if the search turned up anything.

Nancy hadn't said a word during the whole ride back. She was worried. Something felt wrong to her about the planned drop-off of ransom money. She was sure there was a clue she'd missed, but she couldn't figure out what.

One thing was for certain. With Brenda Carlton nosing her way into the case, things would only get more difficult. On top of that, Nancy didn't like the way Brenda had zoned in on David LeGrand.

But the worst thought of all running through Nancy's mind as she drove home was the thought of Sharon Krane. Where was she at that very moment?

Things didn't get any better Sunday morning. As Nancy was finishing breakfast, Bess rang the doorbell. She had a copy of *Today's Times* in her hand. The headline fairly screamed at Nancy: "Famed Psychic on the Case: David LeGrand Finds Clue to Whereabouts of Policeman's Missing Daughter!"

"Oh, brother," Nancy moaned. "She must have gotten her dad to stop the presses to get this information into the paper so quickly." Brenda's father was the publisher of *Today's Times*.

"You need to read it," Bess told her. "You're in it."

Nancy sat down in the living room and skimmed the article quickly. She read all about

how handsome young David LeGrand had succeeded where the police and even the "much-
touted Nancy Drew" had failed miserably.

"Wonderful," she said as she finished. Feeling
nauseated, she put the paper down on the coffee
table.

"Nan, you know you had to read it," Bess said.
"If you hadn't, you'd have been dying of curiosity all day. Now you can get on with your life, and
you know who to strangle the next time you see
her."

"I already knew that part," Nancy said, managing a grin. "You're right, Bess. What do I care
what Brenda writes? The important thing is that
somebody solves the case, whether it's David or
me."

"He is so gorgeous," Bess said. "And it's
obvious he likes you."

"Is it?" Nancy asked, knowing it was true.

"You like him, too, don't deny it!" Bess said.
"I've known you too long."

"Oh, Bess," Nancy said, putting her head in
her hands. "What am I getting into? I've got
Ned, after all. And David's a psychic, of all
things! I don't even believe in that stuff!"

"Hold it right there, Nan," Bess said. "You are
such a skeptic. Listen, you're coming with me to
Madame Tatiana's right now. After she reads
your cards, *then* tell me you don't believe."

"Bess, I—"

"Forget it," Bess overruled her. "You're coming with me. Right now!" Bess grabbed Nancy's hand and pulled her toward the front door.

"Wait, Bess!" Nancy begged. "Isn't George coming back later today? Why don't we wait until—"

"No way!" Bess was not going to give up on this one, Nancy could tell. Resigning herself, Nancy figured if she looked at it as a novel experience, she could get through it.

After Nancy got her shoulder bag, Bess hurried Nancy into her car, and they took off. "That's really something how David found that jacket of Sharon's," Bess said a few minutes later. "How can you not believe in ESP after something like that, Nan?"

"It's not that I don't believe, really," Nancy said. "It's just that I think most of these so-called psychics are total phonies. And even the ones like David . . . well, I think he's following some kind of logic—even if it's a logic neither he nor anybody else understands."

"Well, how about this, then?" Bess asked. "Last night, after the show, I went to see Madame Tatiana. I had my cards read, and she told me my friend was in danger. That doesn't sound like logic to me. And she didn't even know I knew Sharon!"

Nancy frowned. "Maybe she was just guessing. After all, a girl like you would naturally have lots of friends. One of them is probably in some kind of danger—danger of failing a class or losing a boyfriend. Danger can mean almost anything."

"Nancy," Bess said patiently, "Madame meant *danger*. As in life and death, okay? I could tell by the way she said it. Somehow, she must have known about Sharon."

"Well, then," Nancy said with a weary smile, "maybe I *will* learn something after all."

The painted sign in the big picture window said, "Madame Tatiana: Fortune-teller! Readings—Affordable and Accurate! Come in and See Your Future!"

Nancy tried to conceal her amusement as they stepped inside. The fortune-teller's lair was just as she'd imagined it would be—and then some. Madame Tatiana's tiny front parlor was draped in dark, filmy, print fabric, with glass beads curtaining off a door to the rear. A parrot wearing an eyepatch watched them warily from a high wooden perch in one corner.

The girls walked to a pair of overstuffed chairs and sat down.

The glass beads parted, and there stood Madame. She smiled at Bess and went to embrace her. "Dahling," she said, kissing the air near each of Bess's cheeks. "And your charming friend! Hello, Nancy. It is Nancy, am I not correct?"

There was a trace of a European accent in the woman's speech. Nancy took the hand Madame Tatiana offered her and shook it. "Yes, ma'am," she said.

"Call me Madame," said Madame. "Everyone does. So, you come to know your future, Nancy? Of course you do. Pull your chair up to the table." Madame took a velvet pouch from the mantelpiece and removed a deck of cards. She sat down at the table, then spread the cards out on a large piece of velvet cloth. "You must pass your energy onto the cards. Like so."

Madame moved her hands in circles around the cards, humming softly as she did so. Nancy pressed her lips together to keep from giggling.

"Now you," Madame instructed. Hiding a smile, Nancy did as Madame had, humming over the cards.

"Now shuffle the deck, and cut it in three piles."

After Nancy had shuffled the cards and cut them, Madame turned over the top card in each pile. She gasped in astonishment—overdoing it a little, in Nancy's opinion.

"Queen of hearts, queen of diamonds, queen of spades!" Madame whispered dramatically. "Something done for love, something done for money, and a woman in danger!"

"The queen of spades came up in my reading,

too," Bess told Nancy. Turning to Madame, she explained, "Nancy and I both know Sharon Krane, the girl who was kidnapped."

"Aha!" Madame said, her eyebrows lifting until they disappeared under her bangs. "Did I not say you had a friend in danger?"

"Madame," Nancy interrupted. "Did you actually know it was Sharon Krane last night when you made that prediction?"

"Of course I knew! Madame sees all, knows all! The cards do not lie."

"Then where is she?" Nancy asked. "Can you see where she is?"

Madame closed her eyes and hummed for a short while. Then she said, "I see a dark room . . . rubbish . . . I see a denim jacket."

She's seen the newspaper, Nancy realized. Still, before the paper had come out, Madame had guessed that Bess had a friend in danger. Nancy had assumed it was just a vague prediction, which could have been true for anyone. Now she wasn't so sure.

Eyes still closed, Madame put her hands to her temples. "Your friend has a secret . . . something up her sleeve. . . ."

Nancy drew her breath in sharply. There had been nothing in the paper about the note in the sleeve of Sharon's jacket. Was the fortune-teller's figure of speech a coincidence? Or did Madame Tatiana somehow know something?

"Go on, Madame," Nancy said carefully. "What else do you see?"

Madame touched each of the three cards in turn, coming to rest at last on the queen of spades. She opened her eyes. "There is grave danger," she said. "Mortal danger. Where there is now life, there may soon be death."

Nancy felt a chill at the words. She pushed her chair back from the table and rose to her feet. She didn't know whether Madame Tatiana was clairvoyant or not. But her words had reminded Nancy of how little time Sharon might have.

"Thank you, Madame. It's been enlightening. But I have to go," she said. "I have to find my friend, before it's too late."

Madame Tatiana reached out quickly and grabbed Nancy's wrist. The fortune-teller's eyes were wide as she leaned in close to Nancy's face.

"My dear," she said. "You do not understand me. The danger is not only for your friend who has been kidnapped—it is also for *you!*"

Chapter

Seven

Nancy met the fortune-teller's gaze. Was Madame Tatiana's warning based on what the cards had told her? Or did she know of some real danger to Nancy's life?

"Come, sit down," Madame Tatiana said, fluttering her hand. "We will read your tarot. The tarot is a special deck of cards. They will tell us more about the rest of your life—your romantic self. Surely you are in love with someone special? There is a knight in shining armor? Ah, yes, I can tell by the look in your eyes. . . ."

Despite her more serious concerns about Sharon, Nancy found herself blushing. Of course, Ned was the special person in her life, but lately Nancy had been thinking of David LeGrand. His deep-set eyes, his glossy dark hair . . .

"Not today," Nancy begged off, pulling away

from Madame's grip. "Bess and I need to be going."

"We've got time, Nan," Bess said eagerly.

"Maybe you do, Bess," Nancy said, "but I have to find Sharon Krane—and fast."

"You're right," Bess agreed. "Okay. Madame, we'll come back soon. And thank you so much for all your help. We're very grateful. Right, Nan?"

"Uh, right," Nancy said, taking her wallet out of her shoulder bag to pay Madame. "By the way, Madame," she added, "do you happen to remember where you were last Friday night from eleven-thirty on?"

Madame blinked at Nancy and frowned, apparently trying to remember. "I see the future, not the past," she pronounced. "I believe I was here, alone, all night. Why do you ask?"

"Just curious," Nancy said. "Come on, Bess."

"Well?" Bess said when they were on the road again. "What did I tell you? Isn't she amazing?"

"Amazing," Nancy agreed.

"You know, Nan," Bess said, "once or twice in there, I thought you were being rude to Madame. Did I catch you laughing?"

"Me? Laughing?" Nancy protested.

"And why did you ask her where she was Friday night?"

"Bess, I'm still not convinced that Madame's predictions are genuine fortune-telling. Maybe she knew about Sharon some other way," Nancy suggested.

Bess turned to stare at Nancy, then quickly pulled the car over. "Nancy Drew," she said angrily, "are you suggesting that Madame Tatiana kidnapped Sharon? Because if you are, you're out of your mind!"

"Of course I'm not suggesting that," Nancy said. "I just can't figure out how she knew about Sharon—*if* it was Sharon she was talking about when she did your reading last night."

"Well, what about David LeGrand, then?" Bess argued. "He found that jacket, didn't he? Does that mean he's a kidnapper, too?"

"Actually, *I* found the jacket," Nancy corrected her. "Although David did lead us to the spot. To be thorough, though, now that you mention it, Bess, I'm going to check up on David's alibi for Friday night, too."

"Ugh," Bess said. "You are such a skeptic." She put the car back into gear. "Live a little, Nan! Have a little fun. There's more to life than common sense and reason."

Nancy smiled. "You've got me there," she said. "Tell you what, Bess. As soon as I've found Sharon Krane, we'll definitely do something fun—and completely *un*reasonable, okay? You can even take me back for a tarot card reading at Madame's."

"Hmmph," Bess grunted grudgingly. "So, what do you want to do now?"

"I need to go back home," Nancy replied. "I have a lot of stuff to do. Why don't I meet you at George's later?"

"Deal," Bess said.

A few minutes later Bess pulled the car over to the curb in front of Nancy's house. "See you later. And remember what Madame said. Be careful—you're in danger!"

"Right," Nancy said with a smile. "Don't worry about me, okay? *Danger* is my middle name."

The first thing Nancy did was to get in her car and drive to Eddie Hill's neighborhood. There, she talked to a few of Eddie's neighbors, asking them if they had seen him go out or come in Friday night.

But Eddie Hill's neighbors seemed to be a lot like Eddie Hill—hostile, suspicious, and not inclined to talk. Frustrated, Nancy gave up.

She had passed two definite police stakeouts as she drove to and from Hill's neighborhood. Good, she thought. At least Eddie's not going anywhere today without being seen and tailed. Satisfied, she drove downtown.

Her thoughts turned to David LeGrand. Bess had only been defending Madame when she'd brought up David's alibi, but Nancy had promised to check it. Even though she didn't really believe he was a suspect, she pulled over and used a pay phone to call in to police headquarters. Captain Krane, it turned out, had already done a little checking into David LeGrand.

"After he led us to that warehouse, I just wanted to make sure," Krane told Nancy. "So I verified that he checked out of his hotel in Chicago and flew here on Saturday morning. So that's that, Nancy."

Nancy hung up, feeling foolish and a little guilty. Just because *she* didn't believe in ESP didn't mean David LeGrand was a phony. She had read of a number of difficult cases where police had called in psychics.

Suddenly she realized she'd forgotten completely to call David that morning. She got the number of the hotel from information and quickly dialed it, on the off chance that he'd be in his room.

He was. And he was delighted to hear her voice. "Your timing is perfect," he said. "I just got back, and I was about to have brunch. Why don't you join me?"

Half an hour later they were having spinach salad and quiche at the hotel's elegant lobby-level restaurant. Nancy filled him in on her activities, leaving out the visit to Madame's, but including the fact that she'd checked up on his alibi. "You'll be glad to know you're in the clear," she said, giving him a warm smile.

"Whew!" he said, feigning relief. "Lucky me. And good for you for being thorough, Nancy. In your shoes I'd have done the same thing."

"No, you wouldn't," Nancy told him. "You'd have taken one look at me, read my mind, and known I was innocent."

He stared at her, narrowing his eyes. "Innocent?" he joked. "I don't know. . . ."

Nancy laughed. "Seriously, though," she said. "What have you been up to? Any new signals?"

"Actually, yes. I went over to check out Eddie Hill this morning, too—we seem to be on the same wavelength. Captain Krane gave me his address. I didn't feel anything special while I was talking to him—just a vague sense that the man was threatening."

"Vague?" Nancy repeated. "I wouldn't call it vague. He's pretty terrifying, if you ask me."

"Yes, I agree. But Krane told me that there were plainclothes cops staking him out, so I figured I was safe. At any rate, I wanted to check out all the potential suspects."

Then he leaned forward and took her hand in his. "But, Nancy, for the past hour I've been getting signals, on and off. Psychic impulses. I think it's because I've been near the jacket now."

"What kind of signals?" Nancy asked.

"They're like a trail," he explained. "Leading me with images I don't understand."

"Maybe if we drove around again?" Nancy suggested. "My car's just down the block."

He nodded eagerly and took out his wallet to pay the bill. "My treat," he told her. "Can we have dinner as well?"

"Let's see where the investigation is by then," Nancy said.

They left the restaurant and started driving in Nancy's car. She took down the top on the blue Mustang convertible, to give David a better view and a clearer field for him to pick up his "signals."

"That way." He pointed right as they came to a corner. Nancy followed his directions. Again they meandered through town, first this way, then that. It was the same sort of pattern they'd followed when they found Sharon's jacket. Nancy felt herself getting excited, in spite of the fact that she didn't really, in her heart, believe it was possible for David to succeed twice in a row.

"Hey," Nancy said suddenly as they drove through a neighborhood of modest homes. "Tommy Rio lives just over there, beyond those trees."

But David wasn't listening. He was sitting bolt upright in his seat. "Stop the car!" he ordered. Nancy did, and they both hopped out.

This neighborhood was all the way across town from the area where they'd found the jacket and where the police were now concentrating their search. David hurried across the street to a small stand of trees behind a row of houses that included Tommy's. Nancy followed close behind.

Suddenly the psychic dropped to his knees and started creeping around in the brush. "It's so strong!" he gasped. "It's right around here, I know it is!"

Nancy got down on her knees, too. "What are we looking for?" she asked.

"I don't know," he answered. "I hope it's not—"

"Don't even think it," Nancy stopped him. The dreadful thought had occurred to her, too. It was a likely spot to bury evidence—or a body.

"Here!" David suddenly shouted, holding something up, something small and rainbow-colored.

Nancy gasped. "David, you've done it again," Nancy said. "That's one of the earrings Sharon was wearing the night she disappeared!"

Chapter

Eight

NANCY STARED at the earring. The note in Sharon's jacket cuff had been incriminating in an indirect way, but finding Sharon's earring near her ex-boyfriend's house was even worse. Nancy wondered if Sharon had dropped the earring as a clue, hoping, perhaps, that her father might find it.

Nancy stared through the trees toward the back of the Rios' house. She knew that Captain Krane had a surveillance team watching Tommy's movements, but they were probably parked on the street in front of Tommy's house. With these woods behind his house, Tommy could easily sneak out a back window after dark without being seen. She made a mental note to point out this possible escape route to the police.

Both Eddie Hill's house and Tommy's had

been searched by police. So Sharon—if she was still alive—was obviously being held somewhere else, Nancy reasoned. And if that was true, and either Eddie or Tommy was involved, someone else might be guarding Sharon for them.

"What are you thinking?" David asked her.

"I'm thinking we should show Captain Krane the earring right away," Nancy answered. David nodded in agreement, and they both headed back to her car.

When they arrived at police headquarters, they found that the place was a beehive of activity. Everyone seemed energized, especially Captain Krane. He was on two phones, giving instructions to his subordinates for that night's sting operation and shouting questions across the large bullpen area to his fellow officers.

"Is the fake money all set?" he demanded.

"They're working on it upstairs," he was told by a female officer.

"Have they turned up anything at that warehouse?" he asked another officer.

"Not yet," the officer answered. "The place seems clean. He must have just thrown the jacket in the Dumpster there."

Nancy frowned. The warehouse was about as far as you could get in River Heights from Tommy Rio's house. If Tommy had wanted to throw suspicion on someone else, dropping the jacket there would have been a good idea. Of course, that explanation meant he hadn't noticed the note in the cuff—and he would have searched for it, she thought. The note was pretty incriminating. Cuffs were not the normal spot to keep a note, though, and the note was tucked in deep. Tommy might have gone through the pockets and still missed it.

But that didn't explain the earring. Why had it been so close to his own home, when the jacket was so far away? Was he moving her from place to place?

"Hello, Nancy and David," the captain greeted them when he finally hung up both phones. "It's a zoo here. Have you two found anything?"

"This," David said, holding out the earring.

Captain Krane gasped when he saw it. "Where did you get this?" he asked.

"Out in a wooded area behind Tommy Rio's house," Nancy said. "David was getting signals leading him there."

"Tommy, huh?" The Captain fumed. "I'm going to haul that kid in here and make him talk!"

"But, Captain," said a female lieutenant, "what about tonight?"

"Keep it going for me," Captain Krane told her. "I'm going to handle Tommy Rio myself."

While they waited for Tommy to be brought in and questioned, Nancy and David decided to have dinner across the street from the police station.

After they ordered, Nancy sat there, feeling a strange mix of emotions. She felt drawn to David. And, in spite of all her misgivings about his profession, he had again located another crucial piece of evidence.

"You really are something," she told him.

"You're pretty impressive yourself," he said. "You know, I had this fantasy last night that you and I could someday go into partnership . . . solve crimes together." He looked into her eyes and held her gaze for a long moment.

"Well, hello there!" Brenda Carlton's brassy voice abruptly broke the mood. "You've been avoiding me, David," she scolded him as she sat down in a chair between him and Nancy.

"No, honestly," he protested. "I've been heavily involved on the case."

"Do tell," Brenda cooed, pulling her tape recorder out of her bag and switching it on.

David looked at Nancy helplessly, and Nancy shrugged and smiled at him. "It's okay," she said graciously. "I want to get back to police headquarters anyway. I'll ask the waiter to change my order to take-out. See you later?"

He nodded and turned to answer another of Brenda's questions. Nancy shook her head as she went to look for the waiter. Brenda Carlton had more nerve than anyone in the entire universe.

When Nancy returned to police headquarters, she found Krane already interviewing Tommy Rio. Nancy took a seat and waited. A few minutes later Krane emerged from his office, red-faced, and slammed the door.

"The kid's not talking," he grumbled. "Brought a lawyer in here with him, and he's been well coached, too. Searched his house again and the woods, but nothing turned up. I had to let him go."

As he said the words, Tommy and a heavyset older man emerged from the captain's office and walked slowly toward the exit. Tommy looked a little dazed. He glanced at Nancy, then turned his head quickly, following his lawyer out the door.

Captain Krane pounded his fist on a nearby desk in frustration. "Where's my girl, Nancy?" he asked her. "Where in the world is my poor, sick daughter?"

Nancy was worried for Sharon, too. By tomorrow morning at the latest, her supply of insulin would have run out. How would she get more? Insulin was a prescription drug, Nancy knew. And without it, Sharon's life would be in more danger with every passing moment.

Nancy understood why Krane hadn't been able to wait until after that night's sting to bring in Tommy Rio. But she couldn't help feeling now that Krane had made a big mistake. If Tommy was guilty, he certainly wouldn't take the risk of picking up his money tonight in Riverside Park, knowing he was already suspect number one.

Nancy had some time before she had to be back at the station, so she ate her now-cold hamburger platter, then headed over to George's to say a quick hello. Bess had already filled George in on everything that had happened, and Nancy updated them about David LeGrand finding the earring and Tommy Rio being questioned again.

"Wow!" George said. "This guy David sounds pretty amazing!"

"He is," Nancy had to agree.

"Nancy's quickly becoming a believer in ESP," Bess told George with a wink. "I knew she'd come around sooner or later. And with a hunk like David LeGrand around, no wonder it's sooner."

"Give me a break, Bess," Nancy said. "David and I are just working together, that's all."

"Sure, sure. Well, anyway," Bess backtracked, "Nan even went with me to Madame Tatiana's. I never thought I'd get her to come, but she did."

"Oh, and by the way," Nancy said, "I was in no danger at all today, thank you very much."

"Except maybe the danger of losing your

heart," Bess said. "There's more than one kind of danger. Remember?" She nodded knowingly at George.

"So what did you think of Madame?" George asked. "Bess says she's uncanny."

"I'd have to agree with that," Nancy said dryly. "But you know, come to think of it—how would you guys like to help me on this case?"

"How?" Bess asked eagerly.

"Anything we can do to help," George added. "You know we're there for you."

"I was thinking," Nancy said, "since David has managed to dig up so much evidence so fast, maybe Madame could help, too. How would you two feel about getting her involved—in an informal way, at least? Talk to her, see if she can come up with any clues. Who knows—maybe she can use her psychic skills to find Sharon." Nancy couldn't believe she was even suggesting this, but at the moment she was feeling desperate.

"Great idea, Nan," Bess said excitedly. "But you're coming with us, right?"

"I have to get back to police headquarters," Nancy said. "Something's on for tonight—I can't explain right now, but I have to be there for it. Give Madame my best."

Maybe she was becoming more open-minded after all, Nancy thought as she knelt behind a bush in Riverside Park, wearing a pair of night-vision glasses that Captain Krane had given her. If David LeGrand was really psychic, why not Madame Tatiana, too? Just because she was a character didn't mean she wasn't for real, did it? Besides, time was getting extremely short, and Sharon had to be rescued as quickly as possible. Help from any quarter was more than welcome.

David and Captain Krane were stooped down beside Nancy. The captain held a walkie-talkie, with a wire to an earphone in his ear to reduce the crackling sound of the speaker. Silence was crucial. Nothing must alert the kidnapper to their presence in the park.

The counterfeit money, in a clear, plastic bag, sat nearly hidden in the shadows under the tree near the boathouse. Several times people walked by on the adjacent path. But by 12:30 A.M., when no one had come to claim the money, everyone began to get discouraged.

Then the call came in. Krane stood alert, then repeated to Nancy and David what he'd heard over his walkie-talkie. "Eddie Hill just left his house. He's in his car, headed this way!"

Nancy could feel the tension mounting as they waited, silent and fully alert. A few minutes later LeGrand whispered, "Here comes someone!"

A lone figure dressed in black was jogging down Riverside Drive. Through her night-vision glasses, Nancy recognized Eddie Hill. He looked over his shoulder furtively, then jogged into the park, coming right toward them. Except for the lack of a ski mask, he looked an awful lot like the shadowy figure she'd seen in the alley that night.

Eddie ran down to the boathouse, then stopped and looked around. He checked his watch, looked around again, then suddenly turned and began jogging down the path along the river toward the Maple Avenue Bridge. He turned onto it, quickening his pace to a full run.

"Pick up his trail on the other side of the bridge!" Krane ordered into his walkie-talkie. "Well, I'll be. I thought for sure it would be Tommy Rio. What do you think, LeGrand? Is Eddie our man?"

David frowned. "Eddie looked as if he was up to something, all right."

"Definitely," Nancy agreed. "But did you notice—with all his looking around, he never once looked at the oak tree to see if the money was there?"

"Maybe he did, and you didn't notice," Captain Krane suggested.

"No," David said. "Nancy's right. He never looked at it."

"Are you two trying to tell me that Eddie Hill's being here is just a coincidence? That he left his house in the middle of the night, just to come here for his health? If that's a coincidence, it's an awfully big one."

At two in the morning they gave up. Eddie Hill had been tailed all the way back to his house. No one had picked up the ransom money. Sharon remained a captive. And her time was running out, Nancy thought—if it hadn't already.

All the way back to headquarters, Captain Krane sat ashen-faced and silent in the squad car. Nancy could see that he was struggling to keep his composure. The need to save his daughter's life was the only thing keeping Philip Krane together.

"Want to come in for a minute?" he asked Nancy after dropping off David at his hotel. "I know it's late, but—I guess I'm not ready to be alone yet."

"Sure," Nancy said sympathetically, following him inside the headquarters building.

"I'm beyond exhausted," the captain admitted. "You must be feeling it, too, Nancy. I'll let you go in a minute." He opened the door to his office and led her inside. There, he collapsed on a cot that had been set up for him in one corner of the room.

"Do you want a glass of water or something?" Nancy asked him.

"No, thanks," he said.

"What do we do next?" Nancy asked.

"I'm not sure," he said. "Unless LeGrand can lead us straight to Sharon, I don't know what to do. Arresting Tommy and Eddie won't get Sharon back—it might even endanger her life further. Because whoever did this didn't do it alone. Neither Tommy nor Eddie is with Sharon. That means somebody else is. And if I take in Tommy and Eddie, that person might hurt her."

"Right," Nancy agreed. Assuming Sharon was alive, she added silently.

Her mind was fuzzy with fatigue, but for the second time in the past twenty-four hours, Nancy had the distinct feeling that she was missing something—some key point that could crack the case.

Suddenly the phone on Captain Krane's desk broke the silence, and the train of Nancy's thoughts. The captain leaped off the cot and yanked the receiver to his ear. "Hello?" he said anxiously. "Krane here."

As he listened to the voice on the other end of the wire, his face went dead white. He flicked the button on his phone that would tape the message and motioned to Nancy. Covering the mouthpiece, Captain Krane whispered, "Get a trace!"

Nancy ran out of the office and found someone to trace the call. She returned to find Krane standing still as a statue, the phone hanging limp in his hands. "He hung up," he said.

"He?" Nancy repeated. "Who?"

"Listen," Krane told her. He punched a button on the phone and replayed the conversation.

"That was a nasty little trap you set out there tonight, Krane," the voice snarled. "If you try it again tomorrow night, the girl dies, okay? Same time, same place—last chance!"

Chapter

Nine

THE VOICE had been distorted, but both of them recognized the caller. The speech pattern, the gruff tone, were unmistakable. "Eddie Hill!" Nancy and the captain said at the same moment.

There was a knock at the door, and an officer entered, looking excited. "We've traced the call, Captain," the officer said. "It came from the pay phone at Eddie Hill's corner."

Captain Krane hit the desk with his fist. "I want him brought in right now!"

Nancy sat there, trying to make sense of it all. If Eddie Hill was the culprit, had he dropped the earring behind Tommy's house just to throw suspicion on someone else? It made sense, she thought, relieved that, for the moment at least, Tommy Rio seemed to be off the hook. Unless, of course, strange as it might seem, he and Eddie were working together.

Fifteen minutes later Eddie Hill was shown in, in handcuffs and accompanied by two burly sergeants.

"You're harassing me, Krane," he growled. Then he noticed Nancy. "I seen you before. So you're a cop, too, huh? I knew it."

"Shut up, Eddie," Captain Krane ordered. "I want my daughter, and I want her now. Where is she?"

Hill sneered. "I want a lawyer, and I want him now," he shot back. "This is police brutality. Typical, Krane."

Nancy saw that the captain was close to hauling off and socking Eddie in the jaw. But Eddie didn't back off. He seemed to be enjoying Krane's discomfort.

"I'm glad you're hurting, Krane," he said. "You're suffering now the way I suffered all those years because of you. But guess what? I had nothing to do with any of this. I read it in the papers like everybody else. It gave me a warm feeling right here." He looked down at his chest.

"Get this jerk a lawyer," Krane barked, and one of the officers left the room. "You're going to rot in jail, Eddie, if you don't come clean. I'm not letting you out of here until you talk."

"I got nothing to say," Hill retorted. "I'm as

innocent as a rose, okay? You can talk to my lawyer, whoever he is." Still handcuffed, he sat down on a straight-backed wooden chair across from the desk.

This is going nowhere, Nancy thought. She looked up at the office clock and saw that it was now almost three in the morning. All of a sudden a wave of sleepiness washed over her, and she yawned.

"Nancy," Captain Krane said, noticing, "why don't you go on home and get some sleep? I'll call you in the morning."

"What about you, Captain Krane?" Nancy asked, concerned. He'd gotten even less sleep than she had the past couple of days.

"I'll be all right," he told her. "I have to be, for Sharon's sake. You go on ahead. Have someone walk you to your car."

"It's right outside," Nancy told him as she walked toward the door. "I'll be fine. Good luck," she added, with a glance at Eddie Hill.

Nancy got into her car and headed down the deserted avenue. It was a warm, clear night, with a gorgeous full moon, and she enjoyed the soft breeze blowing through the open window as she drove.

She stopped the Mustang at a red light two blocks from the police station. Suddenly she heard a shattering of glass from around the corner. As soon as the light changed, she swung her car onto the side street. Down the block on her right, she could see that the window of a drugstore had been smashed.

Nancy quickly pulled over and shut off the headlights and engine. Just as she was getting out of the car, a masked figure in black jumped back out through the store window. In one hand he held a dark plastic garbage bag; in the other, he had what looked like a flashlight.

He turned to run in Nancy's direction. She stepped out onto the sidewalk to block his path. Seeing her, he stopped dead in his tracks.

Nancy couldn't swear to it, but she was almost sure this was the same man who had been following her and LeGrand after his show the other night. He wore the same black wool ski mask, and had the same large, athletic body.

Abruptly the black-clad figure turned and ran. Nancy took off after him. She wasn't about to let him lose her as easily as he had the last time. She was going to get a good look at this guy's face if it was the last thing she did.

As she chased him around corners and down side streets, she remembered the feeling of missing a crucial element in the case. Now she thought she knew what that element was. It was this masked figure. How did he fit in? Was this the accomplice they'd all talked about?

The figure dashed down an alleyway, and Nancy followed. But the alley ended in an eight-foot-high wire fence. As she entered the alley, Nancy saw the man in black begin to climb. But as he reached for the top of the fence, the bag in his hand fell.

Nancy heard a shattering of glass. The man cursed, shimmied down to get the bag, and quickly climbed up again, then jumped to the ground on the other side just as Nancy got there.

She climbed the fence, but by the time she'd gotten over, the man was gone. She assumed he'd run down an intersecting alley to the street. There was no sign of him.

Now it was Nancy's turn to be upset. She'd been so close, and now she'd lost him. It looked as if she'd have to bring David here to see if he could pick up the guy's trail.

Nancy walked back to the street where her car was parked. There was a small group of people standing in front of the burglarized drugstore now. Nancy went up to them and saw that they were gathered around a man talking to a police officer.

"I'm the pharmacist," the man was saying. "I got the alarm, too, and I came over right away. I only live two blocks from here. Whoever it was must have been in and out in less than a minute."

"He was," Nancy offered. "I happened to be driving by when I heard the window break. I pulled up right over there and saw the guy come out. He was wearing all black, with gloves and a ski mask, and he was carrying a bag of stuff. There must have been glass in it, because while I was chasing him, he dropped it for a second, and I heard glass breaking."

"Sounds as if he knew what he was after," the police officer said. "It wasn't just cash, either."

"He certainly didn't get any cash," the pharmacist said. "I don't leave money around after I'm gone for the night."

The police officer and pharmacist went inside with Nancy right behind them. The rest of the people waited outside.

The druggist quickly searched his shelves. "Doesn't seem as if he took any of the usual stuff, like prescription painkillers," he said. "None of it's been touched."

"Could you check your supplies of insulin?" Nancy asked, playing a hunch.

"Insulin?" the druggist repeated. "Who'd want to steal that?" When Nancy didn't answer, he went over to a refrigerator behind the counter and opened the door.

"Well, I'll be!" he said. "You must be psychic, lady. He cleaned me out. All my insulin supply is gone!"

Chapter

Ten

A THRILL went through Nancy as it hit her—
Sharon Krane was still alive! Why else would her
kidnappers be stealing insulin?

"What about syringes?" Nancy asked.

The druggist checked a drawer. "Yep. A whole
box is missing."

Nancy felt sure that the man in black was
connected with Sharon's disappearance. She still
didn't know why he'd been following her and
David LeGrand that first night after his show,
though. Maybe it was because he knew she was
on the case. But how could he have known? Of
course! she thought. She had talked to both
Eddie and Tommy the morning after Sharon's
disappearance. Maybe one of them had had her
tailed, to stop her from investigating. She shud-

dered as she thought of Madame Tatiana's words: *The danger . . . is also for you. . . .*

But she couldn't worry about that now. She wanted to tell Captain Krane the good news that his daughter was still alive.

As Nancy gave her statement to the officer on the scene, she thought of Tommy Rio. She wondered if he himself had slipped on a black ski mask and gloves and had come here looking for insulin.

But then there was that distorted voice on the phone. The speech pattern and vocabulary were Eddie Hill's, and the call had come from Eddie's neighborhood. But Eddie wasn't the guy in the ski mask because he was at police headquarters, Nancy thought. It could have been one of his low-life friends, though.

Nancy's mind was spinning as she left the drugstore and went to her car. She started the engine and put it in gear. But then she had a thought, a picture, really, of the alleyway where the man had dropped the plastic bag. The shattering of insulin vials . . . sharp glass.

If that sharp glass had punctured that plastic bag, there would be a liquid trail to follow. And if Nancy could find it before it dried out, it might just lead her to Sharon Krane.

There was no time to lose. Nancy said good night to the police officer, got in her car, and drove to the alley. She parked the car at the curb and proceeded on foot to the fence where the man had dropped the bag.

Sure enough, there on the ground at the foot of the fence was a small puddle of clear liquid. Nancy climbed the fence and dropped down on the other side. She pulled her pocket flashlight out of her bag and flashed it around. She spotted several drops of liquid leading down the side alley.

The trail was still there! Nancy exulted in her discovery—the product of logic, not the supernatural, she told herself proudly.

As she followed the trail down the alley, it occurred to her that she should have brought a police escort with her. But there had been no time. Nancy proceeded, looking from left to right, alert to any possible ambush as she searched for droplets of insulin. The trail led to the metal door of a large building at the end of the alley. Nancy tried the door. To her great surprise, it was open. She stopped for a moment to consider her next move. Now would be the time to go phone the police.

But she didn't want to leave the spot. What if her leaving gave the culprit time to get away? Nancy slowly pulled the door open.

She stood in the doorway, waiting for her eyes to adjust to the blackness. She didn't want to use her flashlight, for fear the guy in black was inside. After a few moments the light from the street lamps outside filtered in enough for her to see a large open space with corridors leading off it.

She hesitated, listening. She didn't hear a sound. Taking a chance, she briefly turned on her flashlight and began walking along one corridor. As she went down the hallway, she glanced into the rooms on either side. The doors were open. Most of the rooms were empty, but a few had desks and chairs in them, covered with dust.

In one of the rooms Nancy finally struck paydirt. She flicked on her flashlight and saw a crude cot, with ropes tied to it. Nancy stifled a gasp. Sharon must have been here—and not long ago, either!

As Nancy looked around for more evidence of Sharon's presence, she suddenly heard a sound—the scuffling of footsteps, coming her way.

She turned off her flashlight and retreated into the shadows of the room, hoping that whoever it was wouldn't come in there. She looked around for some kind of object to defend herself with, but there was none.

The footsteps stopped at the door. Nancy held her breath and looked up.

A man was outlined in the doorway. In one hand he held a flashlight, which was pointed toward the floor. In the other hand he held the ski mask he'd been wearing both times Nancy had seen him.

Nancy's eyes had adjusted to the darkness, and in the dim light from the room's only window Nancy could make out his features—a round face with short, peroxide blond hair. Nancy had never seen him before, but she knew she would never forget that face. It had a jagged scar all the way down the left side, from the forehead to the jawbone.

Suddenly he raised his flashlight and shone it on Nancy. "Hey! What the—?"

Nancy didn't give the man time to react. In an instant she sprang at him, giving him a karate chop. The flashlight went flying. The man tumbled backward into the hallway.

Nancy came at him again, using all her martial arts skills. Groaning in pain, the man fell to the ground.

Nancy stepped back to catch her breath. She would get the ropes and tie this guy up, she decided. Then she would call the police, and—

Suddenly a strong arm wrapped itself around her. A gloved hand with a handkerchief in it closed over Nancy's mouth.

"Boss!" the man on the ground moaned. "Am I glad to see you!"

Nancy inhaled a sickeningly sweet smell. Chloroform, she realized as the world spun into blackness.

Chapter

Eleven

NANCY FELT a terrible, stabbing pain in her head as she opened her eyes. She closed them again, and the image came back to her—the arm around her neck . . . the handkerchief over her mouth . . .

Chloroform. Nancy tried to move and realized that the ropes that had been attached to the cot were now tied to her wrists and ankles.

She had no idea how long she'd been here. Hours, probably. Chloroform took a long while to wear off. Nancy realized she must have arrived just as the kidnappers—for she now knew there were at least two—were moving Sharon to another location.

They had probably decided to move her immediately after Nancy had surprised the man in black while he was stealing insulin for Sharon.

And they had probably come back to remove the cot, only to find Nancy. . . .

She wondered how many insulin bottles had survived intact. Enough, she hoped, to keep Sharon alive until she was found.

Where had they taken Sharon? Did they have another location secured in advance? Or were they now improvising?

Daylight was now pouring through the window. Nancy's head ached, but she knew she had to turn her attention to freeing herself. She concentrated on her wrists first. By working them back and forth—a painful process—Nancy finally managed to loosen the rope on her left arm. She set to work untying the other ropes.

Then she heard voices. Someone said, "Nancy." She froze, holding her breath, as the footsteps came down the hallway toward the room.

Nancy let out a sigh of relief as the familiar, welcome face of Captain Krane appeared in the doorway, followed by that of David LeGrand.

"Here she is!" David said triumphantly. "I told you I was getting a strong signal from this building."

The two men rushed to free Nancy, who realized she was still a bit groggy. "Nancy, are you all right?" David asked her.

"I . . . think so," she answered. "Somebody drugged me with chloroform. But I saw the other guy's face."

"Was it Tommy Rio?" Captain Krane asked. "Eddie Hill?"

"Neither," Nancy told him. "A guy with a nasty-looking scar whom I'd never seen before. What time is it, anyway?"

"It's six-thirty in the morning," the captain told her. "Your father called in a panic to say you hadn't come home last night. I had to wake David to help me search for you. It's a good thing I did, too. How did you wind up in this place?"

"I followed the guy here after he stole insulin from the drugstore. They were holding Sharon here," Nancy told him. "I think they were moving her somewhere else when I showed up."

"Did you actually see Sharon?" Krane asked anxiously.

"No," Nancy told him. "But I don't think I could have missed her by more than a few minutes."

Krane frowned. "If Ramirez had called in the insulin theft right away, I would have run down here immediately. As it was, I only found out a couple of hours later."

"I should have had him put in a call to you right away," Nancy said. "I was in too much of a hurry to try to find out where the guy went."

"Completely understandable," Krane comforted her. "Come on, Nancy, let's get you home. You need to get some rest. We all do."

"What about Sharon?" Nancy asked.

"At least we know they tried to get some insulin for her. In a way, I'm glad this happened. You can come in later on and we'll make a composite picture of this guy you saw."

David walked Nancy to her car. "Are you sure you can drive yourself home?" he asked.

"I think so," Nancy said as he helped her into the driver's side. "David, how did you manage to find me?"

"It took a while," he admitted. "We started at the pharmacy, and I followed my instincts, same as usual. I kept coming to this fence at the end of an alleyway, though. It took me a while before we went around and picked up the trail on the other side."

Nancy looked up at him and shook her head in amazement. "How do you do it?"

He returned her smile and stroked her hair softly. "I don't know," he said. "I sometimes think if I try too hard to figure it out, I'll lose the talent. So I just sit back and thank my lucky stars. I thank them for you, too, Nancy. I'm so glad you weren't hurt. You really should be more careful, you know?"

"I know," she said, melting at his touch. "I just couldn't let that guy get away again. I'm sure he was the same one who was following us that first night."

David frowned. "I see," he said. "Okay, Nancy. But next time make sure you have a police escort. Promise?"

"I promise," Nancy said.

"Good." He leaned in and kissed her. Nancy put her arms around his neck, and she leaned back, returning his kiss, feeling herself reeling, not knowing if it was the chloroform or the heady sensation of falling in love.

Nancy awoke to the sound of Bess and George giggling.

"Yoo-hoo, sleeping beauty!" Bess teased. "It's two in the afternoon. Time for Your Majesty to rise."

"Hey, Nan," George said, "did somebody knock you out or something?"

A look from Nancy told George that she wasn't far off the mark.

"Oh!" George exclaimed. "Bess, somebody *did* knock her out!"

"I'm fine, I'm fine," Nancy said, sitting up in bed. "But I've got to get going. I'm losing time."

"Not so fast," Bess said, stopping her. "First you've got to tell us everything. Hannah let us in, then she went shopping. Come on, since Hannah's out, we'll make you some breakfast."

"You mean lunch," George corrected her.

In the kitchen Nancy brought them up to date

while Bess took juice, some fruit salad Hannah had made, and yogurt out of the refrigerator.

"I've got to meet this LeGrand guy," George said when Nancy had finished. "He sounds awesome!"

"Nancy's in love," Bess commented. "Don't say you aren't, Nan, because you can't fool me. And you're gonna love him even more when you check out the morning paper. Brenda Carlton's interview with him is incredible!"

Bess served the newspaper with the fruit and yogurt, and Nancy read all about the great David LeGrand and how he was about to solve another kidnapping. She wasn't even mentioned, Nancy noticed with annoyance. Brenda had really trashed up the article, too, talking about how handsome David was and what he was wearing.

Still, David LeGrand came off very well in his statements, Nancy thought. He seemed both humble and brilliant—just as he did in person.

"Anybody can do what I do," David had told Brenda. "At my final performance in Chicago, last Thursday, one of the volunteers in the audience wound up discovering she had tremendous psychic talent. She could become one of the greatest someday."

Nancy put the paper down and finished her sandwich. She was reaching for her glass of juice when Bess spoke up.

"Okay," she said, "now that you've eaten, it's time for us to tell you what we've been up to."

"Actually, I just tagged along," George said. "Bess did all the talking."

"What talking?" Nancy asked, suddenly curious.

"We've convinced Madame Tatiana to help us on the case," Bess said excitedly. "Isn't that fantastic? And she wants to see you right away, Nan. In fact, that's why we came over here."

"Hmmm," Nancy said. "You know, I wouldn't mind talking to Madame right about now. She knew I was in danger. Either she's as psychic as you say, Bess, or she's a pretty good guesser."

Nancy sat patiently while the fortune-teller went through her routine, laying out the deck of tarot cards and going through all the mumbo-jumbo. At least that's how it seemed to Nancy.

She wondered if the reason Madame had consented to help on the Sharon Krane case was because she'd been reading the paper again and had seen the interview with David LeGrand. She must be burning with jealousy, Nancy realized. She couldn't blame Madame if she was. After all, Nancy had to admit she was a little jealous herself. David had made genuine progress on the case, while all she had done was get herself chloroformed and tied to a bed.

Finally, though, as Madame Tatiana continued to moan over the cards, Nancy ran out of patience. "Madame," she said, standing. "Please. I have to get down to police headquarters and help them draw a sketch of the man I chased last night. My cards can wait for another time. If you really want to help us find Sharon Krane, we have to get to it immediately."

Madame's eyes widened into a look of shocked hurt. "But, my dear!" she said in an offended tone. "I *am* helping you! The cards know all. Sit, please. You'll spoil the vibrations."

Nancy sat, staring down at the table to avoid the angry gaze she knew Bess must be leveling at her.

Madame was silent for a moment, then turned over the cards. "Knight of rods!" she gasped. "Knight of swords and queen of swords! My goodness . . ."

In spite of herself, Nancy couldn't help but feel a twinge of excitement. "What is it?" she asked. "What do you see?"

Madame looked up at her with huge, sad eyes and pouting lips. "You have a boyfriend?" she asked.

Nancy blinked. "Uh, yes," she said. "Why? Does this have to do with Sharon Krane, Madame?"

"It is important," Madame insisted. "Because, you see, there is a deception." She pointed to the knight of rods and the knight of swords, with the queen of swords in between. "The queen is staring at the knight of swords. She does not see his shadow, the knight of rods!"

"Madame," Nancy said, "could you translate please? What are you trying to say?"

"I warned you once, my dear," Madame Tatiana said, her eyes narrowing. "Do not ignore my words again. You are being deceived. Your knight in shining armor is not all you think he is."

Nancy wrinkled her brow in confusion. What was the woman talking about? Nancy had known Ned for years, and he'd always been the same, wonderful guy. She refused to believe that Ned was—

Wait a minute, Nancy suddenly realized. Ned isn't the guy I've been thinking about recently. . . .

She gasped as it hit her. Madame was talking about David LeGrand!

Chapter

Twelve

NANCY SAT rigid, taking in the meaning of Madame Tatiana's words.

Of course, the fortune-teller had every reason in the world to be suspicious of David LeGrand, Nancy realized. He had succeeded where she never had. He had actually helped the police on three separate cases. He was famous beyond Madame's wildest dreams. He was also young, handsome, and swooned over by newspaper reporters. Of course Madame was jealous.

On the other hand, Madame had been right twice before—about a friend being in danger and about the note in Sharon's jacket sleeve. Maybe David LeGrand wasn't all he seemed. Still, Nancy refused to believe he was a fake. If he was, the only way he could have known that the jacket and earring would be there was if he himself was—

No, that couldn't be, Nancy reasoned. He hadn't even arrived in River Heights until Saturday morning. On Friday night he'd been in Chicago, winding up his engagement there. . . .

Suddenly alarm bells were going off inside Nancy's head. Something was wrong. What was it? Something he'd said in his interview with Brenda . . .

Nancy nearly groaned out loud. She'd left the paper at home on the kitchen table. She had to get another look at it and fast. "I—I have to be going," she said, getting up hurriedly.

Bess and George looked at her with concern. "It's okay. I'm all right," she assured them. "But I have to meet with the sketch artist at headquarters. I'll see you two later, okay?"

"But we've got the car," Bess said. "We can drive you over there."

"No, thanks," Nancy told her. "It's only a few blocks. I'll walk. I need to think things over, anyway. Thank you, Madame—it's been enlightening. I'll see you again soon."

Madame nodded as Nancy backed out the door. Two blocks down she found a newsstand and grabbed a paper. She stood in a doorway and opened it to Brenda Carlton's interview.

There it was—the phrase that had troubled

her. David was saying "at my last performance, on Thursday night . . ."

Nancy was sure she remembered him telling her that he'd closed his run in Chicago on *Friday* night. Yes, in the alley outside the theater the first night she'd met him, just before she had discovered the man following them.

Maybe he had just gotten the date wrong. It wouldn't be surprising. After all, he probably did a lot of shows and a lot of touring. And according to Captain Krane, David had flown to River Heights and checked into his hotel on Saturday morning. So what did it matter when his last show was?

Still, it made Nancy wonder. What had he been doing on Friday? Could he have been in River Heights, kidnapped Sharon, then driven back to Chicago and hopped the morning plane back down? It seemed absurd, but it would have been possible, she supposed. And it certainly would have given him an alibi. But why would he kidnap Sharon? Nancy shook her head and threw the paper into a nearby trash basket.

At headquarters Captain Krane was again taking charge of a major sting operation. He took Nancy into his office to give her a brief rundown while she went through mug shots, trying to identify the man who'd robbed the pharmacy.

"This time we're going to get them," he told

her, his jaw set with determination. "I have a quarter million dollars in marked bills from the Treasury Department, and I have reinforcements from all over the county. We're going to leave the park clear this time, but once he comes out, we've got him. I'll have roadblocks at every entrance to this town and a cordon half a mile square under surveillance. Sharon's alive and in River Heights, Nancy. They're not going to get away with this."

"What about Sharon's safety if these guys realize they're trapped?" Nancy asked.

Krane's face grew grim. "We have to hope we can get in there in time and save her. And to make sure we're right on top of these guys, the money bag is rigged. There's a device inside, set to go off within five minutes after the bag is touched. It'll puncture the bag and leave a trail of transparent dye. When you shine a flashlight on it, this dye lights up, like an airport runway at night, and leads us straight to Sharon—I hope before they've had a chance to harm her."

"Sounds like a great idea," Nancy said, then looked down at the book in her lap. "If you don't mind," she added apologetically, "I really need to concentrate on these mug shots."

"No, no, go ahead," Captain Krane said, standing. "I'll check on you in fifteen minutes."

In fifteen minutes the captain was back. Nancy

looked up at him. "It wasn't any of the guys in this book, Captain."

"All right," he said. "Let me bring in my sketch man and you can do a little portrait together."

Nancy watched him go. Captain Krane had to know that he was taking a risk with his daughter's life tonight. Nancy only hoped his desperate measures worked.

By the time she was done at police headquarters, it was almost six o'clock. Nancy headed for David LeGrand's hotel and rang him on the lobby phone.

"Nancy!" he answered in a sleepy voice. "I was just catching some z's. How are you feeling?"

"Like having some dinner," Nancy replied. "Want to come down and join me?"

"Sure thing!" he said. "I'll meet you in the lobby restaurant in ten minutes."

Nancy tried her best to mask her suspicions over dinner. David was being his usual charming self. Nancy asked him a number of questions about himself. He showed no hesitation in answering.

Then she got around to the questions she'd had ever since she left Madame Tatiana's parlor. "David," she said, "tell me about those other cases you helped the police solve. How did they turn out?"

He looked up at her quizzically, then smiled and said, "They worked out fine, actually. In both cases, the missing people were found unharmed."

"Who were they?" Nancy prodded.

"Well, the first was a woman of about thirty, by the name of Gloria Williamson. She was kidnapped from her house. I tracked her from there, found a note she'd written and a shoe, and eventually the place where the kidnappers had hidden her. The other was a young girl about Sharon's age, Valerie Wu. It was more difficult with her because her kidnappers kept moving her around. But in the end we tracked her down."

"You mean *you* tracked her down," Nancy corrected him.

"Well, the police and I," David said with a shrug. "I think the kidnappers just ran out of hideouts."

Nancy found it hard to believe that David LeGrand was anything other than sincere in his concern for the victims he'd helped to rescue. She began to regret ever suspecting that he was not what he seemed to be.

Just then the headwaiter came over to their table. "Telephone call for Mr. LeGrand."

David looked at Nancy. "I'm sorry," he said.

"I've been expecting an important call, so I told them at the front desk I'd be here."

"Right this way, sir," the headwaiter beckoned. David followed him to the lobby.

A few minutes later he returned. "I feel terrible, Nancy," he said, "but I have some business to take care of, and it can't wait. Will you forgive me?"

In spite of his disarming tone, Nancy felt herself growing suspicious again. "Where do you have to go?" she asked. "Maybe I could drive you."

"No, thanks," he said with a smile. "It's quite a ways out of town. I might not be able to get back till tomorrow. You need to be here tonight for the drop-off, don't you? Please give my apologies to Captain Krane. I'll check in with him tomorrow. I hope he'll have the case solved by then."

"No, David, really," Nancy insisted, trying to gauge his reaction. "I don't care if it's a long ride. I want to be with you."

For a split second Nancy thought she detected a flicker of panic in David's eyes. "Well, I guess I'm being driven, then," he said with a shrug. "Just let me make a quick phone call. If the waiter comes by, have him put dinner on my bill. Suite four-thirteen."

Nancy called for the waiter and followed

David's instructions. She checked the time. It was seven-thirty. Plenty of time to get back by midnight.

And even if she didn't, Nancy told herself, Captain Krane probably wouldn't need either one of them for his operation. He had both Eddie Hill and Tommy Rio under surveillance, and he had a sketch of the guy Nancy had followed. She just wanted to make sure David wasn't mixed up in this thing. The only way to do that was to stick with him until the police operation was over.

Nancy checked her watch again. Seven thirty-five. Where was he, anyway? Alarmed, Nancy headed out to the lobby. There was no sign of David. She knocked on the men's room door but got no answer.

Then she saw another door. It led to the basement parking lot, and she saw that it was slightly ajar.

She had a sickening feeling that David Le-Grand had given her the slip.

Chapter
Thirteen

NANCY STEPPED through the door and walked down the steps to the parking garage. She checked the cars, but there was no sign of David's rental car. She ran back up the stairs and was hurrying toward the front door when she heard the headwaiter calling her.

"Miss! Miss!" he said, waving a piece of paper in his hand. "Mr. LeGrand said to give you this."

"He told you to—" Nancy stopped in midsentence, took the letter, and read it, frowning.

"'Nancy,'" she read, "'I'm sorry I have to duck out on you like this, but I'll explain everything when I get back. I got a great lead on the case. Sorry I couldn't take you with me, but I've got to show up alone. Can't wait to see you tomorrow. Love, David.'"

What was he up to? Nancy wondered. Was

David trying to solve the Sharon Krane case on his own, through some secret channel neither she nor the police knew about? Had she judged him too harshly? Or was there something more sinister going on?

Whether David was a hero or a criminal, Madame Tatiana had been right again. There *had* been more to Nancy's shining knight than met the eye. It was time to talk to Madame Tatiana again. But there were other things to take care of first.

Nancy stopped in at police headquarters, to check on the preparation of the midnight drop. Krane took her over to a large table with a map of River Heights spread out on it. The map had different color pins stuck in various places, most in the area near the river and Riverside Park.

"These red pins are our lookout stations—our 'spotters,'" Captain Krane explained. "You'll notice that they're all outside the park, covering the entrances, with the widest possible field of view. We also have spotters on Eddie Hill and Tommy Rio. But something tells me it's the accomplice—the guy in black—who'll be picking up the loot."

Nancy nodded. If Eddie or Tommy was guilty, they were also well aware of the police department's interest in them. And neither one was stupid.

"By the way," Captain Krane told her, "Eddie claims he went to the park last night to meet a friend who never showed up. He won't say who or why, and I don't guess we can make him— yet."

Krane cleared his throat and got back to business. "The blue pins are our roadblocks," he continued. "We've set up a ten-square-block perimeter around the park, and on the other side of the river, too. We've also set up an outer rim of roadblocks at all the entrances to town."

He looked at Nancy and managed a smile. "They can get their money all right," he said. "But they're not going to get out of town with it. You and I are going to watch from this lookout, Nancy. We can see the oak tree and the boathouse from there, and the part of Riverside Drive nearest to it. I've set up three scopes, so you and David can each have one for yourselves. You've both put in a lot of hard work, and you deserve front row seats."

"About David," Nancy spoke up. "I have to talk with you. Alone," she added, glancing around meaningfully.

"Come on in the office," Captain Krane said, leading her away from the crowded table.

Inside his office Nancy told Krane about David's disappearance and her suspicions that he might be involved in Sharon's kidnapping.

Captain Krane looked at her in disbelief.

"Look, Nancy," he said. "It does kind of surprise me that he's not going to be around tonight. He might have come in handy in tracking these guys. But LeGrand has already been a big help more than once."

"That's just it, Captain," Nancy said. "How did he know those things would be there? The jacket? The earring? Even me, in that deserted building? Maybe he *is* psychic, but what if he isn't?"

"If he isn't, there would be only one logical explanation." The captain frowned. "But I don't buy it, Nancy. We were both there when he led us to the jacket. Did it seem to you that he was faking it?"

"No, definitely not," Nancy had to admit. "But remember, Captain Krane, that's just what makes a really good faker."

"Sorry, Nancy," Krane said. "You haven't convinced me. First of all, I already have two strong suspects in this case—Eddie Hill and Tommy Rio. Either one of them could be mixed up with this guy with the scar. We're scanning the computers right now to find a prison connection with Eddie from the sketch you gave us. It's just a matter of time before we link them up."

Captain Krane stood up and went to the door. "Besides, LeGrand's got a great reputation for solving just this kind of kidnapping."

He shook his head and reached for the doorknob. "I'm sorry, Nancy. You've got no proof at all against LeGrand—just supposition. And as for him running off—what if he's working on the case from some other angle?"

"That *did* occur to me," Nancy said.

"Well, then, let's leave it right there," Captain Krane said. "LeGrand can explain himself when he gets back."

He opened the office door. As they entered the main room, there was a commotion at the front door of the building. Three or four police officers were bunched together, trying to keep somebody out.

"I have a right to know what's happening!" Brenda Carlton screeched. "The public has a right to know what the police department is doing to find Sharon Krane! I demand to speak to Captain Krane and Chief McGinnis!"

The knot of officers walked Brenda back outside, trying to calm her down. Nancy couldn't suppress a smile. Poor Brenda, she thought. The greatest story of her career, and the police won't let her in.

But the truth was, Nancy wasn't annoyed at Brenda anymore. After all, it had been Brenda's article that had alerted Nancy to the one piece of evidence she had against David: He hadn't told the truth about the day of his last show in

Chicago. And if he had lied about one thing, what else had he lied about?

The operation went into action at eleven that night. The spotters all assumed their hiding places, but the roadblocks would not go into effect until the money was actually picked up. Then, and only then, would the trap be sprung.

At about twelve-thirty a dark car slowed to a crawl on Riverside Drive. It came to a stop just off the path that led from the road down the slope to the boathouse. It was the narrowest part of the park.

The driver's-side door opened, and out came the now-familiar black-clad figure. He was not wearing his mask. Nancy would never forget that horribly scarred face as long as she lived.

The man in black approached the bag of money cautiously, looking around to make sure it was safe. Then he quickly grabbed it, ran back up the hill to his car, gunned the engine, and took off, burning rubber as he went.

"Roadblocks, take your positions," Captain Krane ordered into his walkie-talkie. He and Nancy both watched the car through scopes. "He's turning onto Neville," Krane announced.

"Roger, Captain. We'll pick him up when he comes past the intersection at Darlington Avenue."

Krane turned to Nancy and gave her a wink. "We've got him now. All we have to do is follow him back to Sharon."

There was a sudden, sharp crackle on the walkie-talkie. "Captain, this is one-two-four. The car hasn't shown up at the corner. He must have pulled over on Neville."

"Bingo!" the captain shouted. "Okay, everyone, pull in the net. Close off everything within ten blocks of the area."

He turned to Nancy and checked his watch. "The device in the money bag should be going off right about . . . now. Come on, Nancy, let's get down there. He can't have gone more than a few blocks."

As they drove down Neville, they spotted the dark car surrounded by a number of unmarked police cars. The captain pulled up to the curb, and he and Nancy got out. "It's a stolen vehicle, Captain," one officer said.

"It figures. Did any other cars come out either side of this block?" Captain Krane asked.

"No, sir," the officer replied. "From here, he went on foot."

"Have you found the dye trail yet?" the captain asked.

"No, sir," said the officer. "Not yet."

"Okay, everyone!" Krane yelled into his walkie-talkie. "We're on the lookout for a man with a long scar down the right side of his face. Don't let him get away. Come on," he told Nancy and a group of officers around her. "We're going to follow the trail to my little girl."

With half a dozen flashlights playing on the pavement, they soon found what they were looking for. The glowing dye trail led them across the street, through an alley, down three more residential blocks, up a driveway, and behind a two-car garage.

Captain Krane nodded, a satisfied look on his face. "You," he pointed to two young officers. "Go behind the garage on the right, and the rest of us will take the left side."

They all ran behind the garage, but a rude shock awaited them. On the ground by the back wall was the black outfit the criminal had worn, along with his black sneakers. Next to the discarded, dye-stained clothes was the plastic bag. It, too, had dye all over it.

"He changed clothes," Krane said, in frustration. "Wouldn't you know the louse would carry a change of clothing with him?"

One of the other police officers was bent over the bag, carefully opening it with a nightstick. "Looks like all the money's inside," he said, standing. "Guess he realized the money wouldn't do him much good, covered with dye like that."

"We have to find him!" Krane said through gritted teeth. "He may kill Sharon out of anger over not getting the money. There must be traces of dye still on him. We need to pick up his trail, and fast!"

Nancy spotted something small and strangely shaped on the ground. She picked it up and examined it. It was long and thin and made of latex rubber—and it smelled of makeup.

"What have you got there, Nancy?" Captain Krane asked.

"I'm not sure," Nancy said. "But it looks a lot like the scar I saw on the guy's face."

"You mean—" Krane's face had gone ashen.

"That's right," Nancy said, nodding. "The scar was a fake."

The search proved fruitless. No more traces of dye were found. The trail had gone cold. The police kept the roadblocks in place, but Nancy had her doubts about how effective that would be. The people they were facing were cunning as well as ruthless. And now they were bound to be furious, too.

Captain Krane was devastated. He was sure he'd succeeded only in further endangering his daughter.

Nancy did what she could to comfort him. Then she went home, hoping that despite her concern and frustration, she could catch a few hours of sleep before getting back on the case.

* * *

Nancy called in to headquarters in the morning. She was told that nothing had turned up yet, but that the search was continuing.

Nancy hurriedly dressed. There were two stops she wanted to make that morning. Madame Tatiana's was one, but first Nancy stopped off at the main branch of the River Heights Public Library.

She headed straight for the microfilm section and started going through files of old newspapers. Soon she found what she was looking for—news stories detailing the role David LeGrand had played in those two earlier kidnapping cases.

She learned that in both cases, as in Sharon's, the victims had come from families that didn't have a lot of money. Strange, Nancy thought. Kidnappers didn't usually choose their victims from families of modest means—unless their motive wasn't money. Both Eddie Hill and Tommy Rio had personal motives, she knew. But if it was unusual to kidnap people who weren't rich, the fact that it had happened in all three of LeGrand's cases was more than unusual—it was downright suspicious.

In both previous cases LeGrand had found several clues and finally discovered the victim. But in neither case had the police made any arrests! Definitely suspicious, Nancy decided.

Suddenly she was struck by a powerful hunch.

Nancy went over to the library's computer and entered the keyword *LeGrand*. Several articles were listed, some even earlier than the two kidnappings. She called these up, and in a photo accompanying one of the articles, she struck paydirt.

The article was about one of LeGrand's earlier shows. The photo showed him with a group of people who were identified in the caption as his assistants.

Nancy stared at the assistant on LeGrand's right. She had seen that face before—and although it had been in the dark, with a fake scar on it, in her heart Nancy was sure.

David LeGrand's assistant was the man in black.

Chapter

Fourteen

Now THERE WAS no doubt in Nancy's mind. David LeGrand was in on the kidnapping of Sharon Krane. She thought back over the case.

The man in the alley after LeGrand's show? He could have been waiting there to catch David on his way out, not to spy on him but to talk to him—to break the disastrous news that Sharon Krane was diabetic.

The fact that Eddie Hill had shown up in Riverside Park that night? Well, hadn't LeGrand told her he'd gone to see Eddie that day? What if he'd managed to lure Eddie to the park somehow, promising to meet him there and get him in on something good?

And the phone call Eddie had made to police headquarters? David could have been the caller—if he'd picked up on Eddie's speech patterns when he saw him. Nancy remembered the distorted quality of "Eddie's" voice on the phone. It could have been a good imitation. And LeGrand was good at a lot of things.

What about his alibi? Nancy was ready to believe by now that he had come to River Heights, helped kidnap Sharon, then doubled back to catch the morning plane. The whole thing fit perfectly with David's careful personality. Sharon's diabetes must have come as quite a shock to him.

Remembering how stunned David had seemed when Captain Krane told him about the diabetes, Nancy felt sick. She made one last, desperate attempt to think of an explanation. There was none. David LeGrand had deceived her. And, just like everyone else, she had fallen under his spell.

Well, her eyes were open now, and it was her turn to make some magic.

Nancy knew that all she had so far was supposition—and her belief that the man in the photo was the man with the scar. That wouldn't be enough to make a case against David, but it might be enough to convince Captain Krane.

Before seeing him, though, there was one more person she wanted to see. Nancy needed to know what, if anything, Madame Tatiana Dove knew. So, after photocopying the articles and photograph, she got back into her car and headed for Bess's house.

Bess and George were both there. "We've been trying to reach you for two hours," Bess complained. "Where have you been?"

"Out investigating," Nancy told them.

"You mean they still haven't found Sharon yet?" George asked, a worried look on her face.

"No," Nancy said. "Listen, you guys, you're not going to believe this—but I think David LeGrand's the guy we're after."

"What?" George gasped.

"You've got to be kidding, Nan!" Bess protested.

"I'm afraid not," Nancy said sadly, and proceeded to tell them the whole story of the past twenty-four hours. Bess and George sat spellbound. "And to think," Nancy concluded, "I was really attracted to the guy."

Silently, both her friends rose and put their arms around Nancy. "Oh, you guys," Nancy said, returning the hug. "You're the absolute best—did I ever tell you that?"

"You don't have to," George assured her. "We already know it."

Nancy smiled. "Now, let's get going. I want to see Madame Tatiana again, right away."

"Yes!" Bess said, clapping her hands. "At last, you've seen the light."

"I have, Bess," Nancy agreed. "I definitely, positively have."

Madame Tatiana greeted them at the door of her salon. The smell of incense wafted all around her. "Come in, come in," she greeted them, arching her eyebrows. "I knew that you would come."

Nancy made a face as she and her friends went inside. She'd had just about enough of the supernatural world.

"Madame," Nancy began when the fortune-teller settled down opposite Nancy on a mountain of embroidered cushions. "I came to see you again because I need to know *how you know.*"

Madame seemed taken aback by Nancy's words. "I do not understand," the fortune-teller said, putting her hand to her throat. "The cards tell me all. Whatever I know, I know because of them."

"No, Madame," Nancy said. "I'm afraid that's not good enough. Not anymore. Someone's life is at stake. You told me my knight in shining armor wasn't what he seemed. You meant David Le-Grand, didn't you? How did you know about him? And please don't try to tell me you saw it in the cards."

"I have never been spoken to like this in my entire career!" Madame Tatiana exploded.

Nancy realized she might be pushing Madame, but she reminded herself that she had a good reason. Sharon's life was the only important thing now.

"I tell you," Madame continued, "true psychics are in tune with the infinite, with the mysteries of the cosmos."

"And David LeGrand, according to you, is not a true psychic?" Nancy pressed.

"He is a charlatan!" Madame said emphatically. "The newspapers love him because he is handsome and young, but he is nothing, I promise you."

"Madame," Nancy said quietly but firmly, "it wasn't the cards that told you David LeGrand was a fake. The police will be interrogating you very soon, and then you'll have to tell it to them. I suggest, for your own sake, you be honest now."

Madame stared at Nancy, then heaved a sigh. "Oh, all right," she said, collapsing back into her cushioned throne. "You're right. The cards didn't tell me about him. I recognize his tricks because I've known other false psychics who use them. He is simply much better at it than most."

Nancy nodded her head slowly. "These other false psychics, Madame. We'll need names, so we can get firsthand information."

"Well," Madame said, dropping any last pretense, "even *I* have resorted to such tricks once or twice in the past. In the *distant* past, mind you. Now I use only the cards and my intuition. But if I must, in court, I can show how such tricks are done."

Nancy glanced at Bess, who scowled and folded her arms in front of her.

"Thank you, Madame," Nancy said, getting up and heading toward the door. "You've done the right thing." Bess and George followed Nancy out, and they all piled into the Mustang.

"I can't believe you!" Bess said as Nancy pulled out into traffic. "I can see why you had to do it, but did you have to be so rude to Madame?"

"I'm sorry, Bess," Nancy said sincerely. "I was only doing it for Sharon. I didn't believe Madame would tell the truth otherwise."

"Well, just because she used some phony tricks in the past, doesn't mean she's a fake now," Bess insisted. "Right, George?"

"Oh, don't put me in the middle of this," George protested, holding up both hands. "I'm neutral, okay? Strictly neutral. Let's change the subject. Where are we headed now?"

"Police headquarters," Nancy told them. "I want to see Captain Krane and show him the articles on David LeGrand. I hope the captain will order a search of David's hotel room. Maybe we'll find something there."

"Sharon?" George asked. "Nancy, you don't think—not right there in his hotel room! How would he even get her up there?"

"He's a brilliant performer, George," Nancy said flatly. "If he wanted to get her up there, I'll bet he'd think of a way. David's very good at getting people to see what he wants them to see. And remember, he had help. Judging by the scar, his assistant is pretty good at disguises."

They pulled into the lot at police headquarters and went inside.

As soon as they got through the outer doors, Nancy and her friends found themselves engulfed in an uproar of activity. Police officers were racing to answer telephones, waving message pads in the air.

"Chief McGinnis!" Nancy shouted to her old friend. "What's going on? Where's Captain Krane?"

"He's down at the hospital," McGinnis said. "They've found Sharon."

"That's fantastic, Chief!" Nancy said excitedly. Then she noticed the grave look on his face. "Or isn't it?"

"I'm afraid not," the chief replied. "They found her lying outside the emergency room, unconscious. Sharon's in a diabetic coma, Nancy. She may not recover."

Chapter

Fifteen

$\mathbf{T}$HE GIRLS DROVE to the hospital, which wasn't far from the police station, with Chief McGinnis. He pulled to a stop outside the emergency room doors, and a crowd of reporters and camera crews—from Chicago as well as local stations—immediately gathered around the chief.

At the head of the crowd stood Brenda Carlton. Nancy was sure that Brenda would somehow manage to get her face on national TV.

"Miss Krane was found right here, where I'm standing, at around five-thirty A.M.," Chief McGinnis was saying. "The ER staff heard a car horn honking outside. When they went to investigate, the car had gone, and Sharon was lying there, unconscious."

"What's her condition, Chief?" one of the reporters shouted.

The chief looked flustered for a moment. Then a doctor came over to him and whispered something in his ear. The chief nodded and broke into a smile.

"Miss Krane was in a diabetic coma when she was admitted," the chief replied. "But I've just been told she's out of danger and is expected to make a full recovery."

"Any leads on the kidnappers?" another reporter asked.

"Yes, we're following up many avenues of investigation," the chief said.

Nancy motioned to Bess and George, and they went inside. They were stopped by the police who were guarding the lobby doors. When Nancy identified herself, the officers let them through and even directed them to the third floor, where Sharon had been admitted to the intensive care unit.

Captain Krane was in the third-floor lounge when Nancy and the girls got there. He was talking on his walkie-talkie to the men posted downstairs. He smiled wearily when he saw the girls.

"Nancy!" he greeted her. "It's a miracle, isn't it?" Then he looked flustered. "I'm so sorry I didn't call you, especially after all your help. But—"

"I understand completely," Nancy said. "And

I'm so glad she's going to be all right." Her feelings were echoed by George and Bess.

"Did she say anything about the men who kidnapped her?" Nancy asked.

The captain shook his head. "She's been too weak and dazed. But it's been about half an hour since I was in there. Maybe we could try her again now."

While Bess and George waited in the lounge area, Nancy went with Captain Krane. He swung open the door to the intensive care unit. "Could we see Sharon?" he asked the head nurse.

"Yes, I think so," the nurse replied, smiling. "She's much better, Captain Krane. It's amazing, considering all she's been through. She came out of the coma very quickly. The doctor says she could be released by tomorrow if she keeps up this progress."

"That's wonderful news," the captain said. "I'm so grateful to all of you."

"Please don't stay long, though," the nurse cautioned them. "Sharon really needs to rest."

"Of course," Krane agreed, leading Nancy in.

Sharon Krane lay in bed with her eyes closed, one arm hooked to an IV tube. Her skin was waxen, and little beads of sweat stood out on her forehead and upper lip. Nancy felt a pang of sorrow, remembering how vibrant Sharon had looked at the party the night she'd been kidnapped.

As they approached, Sharon opened her eyes. "Hi, Daddy," she whispered, trying to smile.

"Honey," Captain Krane said, taking her hand in his, "I brought Nancy Drew with me. She's been helping us try to find you."

Sharon nodded and smiled up at Nancy. "Sharon," Captain Krane went on, "can you tell us what happened? It's important, sweetheart. It might help us find the men who kidnapped you."

A tear trickled from Sharon's eye. "I was walking home from the party," she told them. "I was alone. Tommy and I had a fight, and . . ."

Sharon faltered, and her father said, "Yes, we know about the fight. Then what happened?"

"A car pulled over in front of me on the road. I thought someone from the party wanted to give me a lift. So I walked over to it. I should have known better, but . . . Anyway, all of a sudden, this guy gets out and puts a handkerchief over my mouth."

Nancy nodded, remembering her own attacker. "Did you get a look at him?"

"Yes. He had a terrible scar on his face," Sharon said. "There was someone else around when I woke up, but they had me blindfolded by then. I just heard the two of them talking."

"The scar was false, by the way," Nancy said. "Do you think, if we showed you a picture of the man, but without the scar, you'd still be able to identify him?"

She showed Sharon the newspaper photo of David LeGrand with his assistant. "Is this the man?" she asked, pointing to the assistant.

"I don't know," Sharon said, after studying the photo. "It could be, but I'm not sure. The light wasn't very good in the first place they took me."

"That must be where I got attacked," Nancy told the captain. "Where did they take you after that, Sharon?"

"I don't know," Sharon said. "I'd been without insulin so long that I got sick and passed out. When I came to, I was blindfolded again. But I was in a comfortable bed, not like the first one."

"What about the insulin?" Nancy asked her.

"I had only two vials with me when they took me," Sharon said. "The guy with the scar was pretty upset when he found out I was diabetic. I heard him through the door of my room, talking to some other guy about my diabetes," Sharon went on. "They didn't realize how loud they were talking, I guess. They sounded pretty panicked. The guy with the scar was going to get me some insulin. I don't know how, though, because I didn't have my prescription with me.

"Anyway, he came back with the insulin, but by then I was already pretty sick, and I think most of the vials got broken, because I heard the other one say he'd have to get some more right away. Next thing I knew, the man with the scar was putting that handkerchief to my face again. . . ." Sharon fought back tears.

"After a while in the new place I started to get sick again. I needed the insulin. The man with the scar tried to give me a shot, but I didn't trust him. I know my exact dosage, and I wanted to inject myself, like I had done before. I was thrashing around, and I accidentally hit the vial. It broke, and he yelled at me and called me stupid. He said that was the last vial he had—and then I don't remember any more."

"I see," Nancy said, thinking of David Le-Grand's disappearance. Was that where he'd gone? To get more insulin? Then why had Sharon been returned in the meantime? Had the other man panicked when she went into a coma, dropped her at the hospital, and fled town?

The head nurse came in and signaled that it was time for Captain Krane and Nancy to leave. "We'll let you sleep, Sharon," her father said, kissing her on the forehead.

When they were in the hallway, the captain turned to Nancy. "What's this picture you've got?"

Nancy showed it to him. "That's the man with the scar," Nancy said, pointing to him. "I could swear to it."

"David LeGrand's assistant? Nancy, you brought this up once before, and I told you what I thought. Are you prepared to swear to it in court? Because you heard what Sharon just said. She wasn't sure it was him."

Nancy stood firm. "Captain, I've thought about it a lot, and it all fits. Look, you had surveillance on both Eddie Hill and Tommy Rio last night. Did either one drive Sharon to the hospital?"

"No," Krane said. "Neither one left his house, either early this morning or when the money was picked up. Of course, that doesn't let them off the hook, since the money was probably picked up by an accomplice. They're the only ones with real motives. Remember, Nancy, I'm not a rich man. No professional kidnapper would have chosen my daughter as his victim. As for David LeGrand, he has a lot more money than I do! What possible motive could he have?"

"Fame," Nancy answered. "Think about it, Captain. He's built his reputation, not only on his shows, but on his record for finding kidnap victims. I looked it up, and in each of his previous cases, the victims were found unharmed, but the perpetrators were never apprehended."

"So?" the captain asked.

"So, every case he solves makes David Le-Grand a hotter commodity," Nancy explained. "If the victims died, it wouldn't do him any good."

Captain Krane frowned. "Then how do you

explain Sharon's getting dumped here this morning?" he challenged her. "If your theory's true, shouldn't LeGrand have led us to Sharon, just as he did in the other cases?"

"Yes," Nancy admitted. "But I think that's because something went wrong. I think Sharon went into a diabetic coma while the man with the scar was watching her and David was off trying to get insulin. I think Scarface panicked and dumped her here. Maybe he thought she'd die on him before David got back."

The captain sighed. "Look, Nancy," he said, "this news photo is years old. There's nothing to connect the two of them anymore. Why don't we wait until LeGrand gets back and let him explain things? Maybe it's all perfectly innocent."

He put an arm around Nancy's shoulder. "Listen, you've done a terrific job," he told her. "And I wouldn't blame you a bit if you were upset about all the attention LeGrand's been getting."

"Is that what you think?" Nancy said, stepping away from him. "That I'm jealous of David and that's why I'm accusing him?"

"I didn't say that," Krane said. "But you know how it is, Nancy. When we want to believe something's true, the evidence seems a little more compelling."

Nancy shook her head in frustration. "At least get a search warrant for his hotel room," she ꜱᵈᵉd. "If we find something—some evidence that Sharon's been there or some dye from the money—we can arrest him and wrap up the case right there."

Now it was the captain's turn to shake his head. "I can't allow that, Nancy. David Le-Grand's a celebrity. And he's been a great help to the force on this case. I can't just treat him like a criminal. How would that look in the papers? Besides, if he's as crafty as you say he is, I'm sure he's cleaned up his room."

"Not necessarily," Nancy pressed. "He may not have had time."

At that moment they were interrupted by the head nurse, who told Krane there was a phone call for him. Krane went off to answer it, and when he came back, he had a smile on his face.

"Guess who that was?" he asked Nancy. "David LeGrand! He's on his way back from Chicago, and he'll be here on the next commuter flight. He was mighty glad to hear about Sharon, too. He called first at the station, and they told him I was here. So," he concluded, "in an hour he'll be here, and you can ask him whatever questions you like."

Commuter flight? Nancy thought. Although he hadn't said so directly, David had led her to believe he was taking a long drive. Yet another lie, she thought. But she didn't have time to think about that now.

"An hour? Then we don't have much time,"

Nancy said. "Please, Captain. Trust me on this one thing—you won't regret it."

"I'm sorry, Nancy," he said. "I'm not going to get a search warrant without just cause."

"So that's it?" Nancy asked incredulously. "Sharon's back, so you're just going to let the kidnappers get away with it?"

"I didn't say that," Krane protested. "We're still after those dye traces, and we've erased the scar from the artist's sketches. If we get the guy, we'll make him identify his partner."

"And if you don't?" Nancy asked.

"Nancy, as you said, we've got Sharon back," the captain said firmly. "No money's been lost. If we get our man, fantastic. If not—well, we did our best, and things could have turned out a lot worse."

"And how long do you think it'll be before they kidnap someone else's daughter?" Nancy blurted out. "Captain, just say for a minute that I'm right—David LeGrand's motive doesn't begin and end with you, the way Eddie's or Tommy's does."

Krane sighed. "Look, Nancy," he said. "I'm grateful for all your help. But without something more concrete, I can't get a search warrant for LeGrand's hotel room. If you want to pursue your theory, I'm afraid you're on your own."

Nancy gritted her teeth and walked back to the lounge alone to pick up George and Bess. She could just see how it would all end. The captain was going to declare the case "unsolved," and David LeGrand was going to get away with it.

Nancy promised herself she was not going to let that happen. Somehow, some way, she was going to stop that man once and for all.

But how? She had so little time. How was she going to get into David LeGrand's hotel room? And if she couldn't, how could she get him to incriminate himself?

She walked into the lounge toward her old friends—and suddenly it all became clear. Maybe there was a way after all. But she had to hurry—there wasn't a moment to lose.

Chapter

Sixteen

THE PLAN was wild, definitely a long shot, but something about it felt right to Nancy. Besides, it was her last, best chance to nail David LeGrand. She had to take it.

Not only had he engineered Sharon's kidnapping and endangered her life, but he'd made a fool of Nancy. She'd been so attracted to him that she put aside her wariness about psychic phenomena. She'd actually believed his special powers had led them to Sharon's jacket and earring!

Now she had one last chance to make sure David LeGrand got what he deserved.

"George . . . Bess," Nancy said to her friends. "I'm going to set a trap for David LeGrand, and I need you to help me."

"Anything," Bess said. "He gives people like Madame a bad name."

"I want you to go right over to Madame's, as a matter of fact," Nancy said. "We're going to need her in on this. And you'll have to convince her to play along. Do you think you can do that?"

"No problem," Bess said. "The only thing is, well—I think she might be kind of mad at you, Nan. You know, after last time."

"Oh, right." Nancy suddenly remembered the way she'd embarrassed the fortune-teller. "Please, send her my sincerest apologies, okay, Bess?"

"Why don't you tell her yourself?" Bess asked.

"I have to go to the airport," Nancy told her. "If this is going to work, I can't let David LeGrand out of my sight even for a minute. Now, here's what we're all going to do. . . ."

"Nancy! What a surprise!" David exclaimed as he walked into the terminal and found her waiting.

"An unexpected pleasure?" Nancy asked, keeping her tone light.

"Uh, yes, of course!" he said, a bit nervously. Nancy noticed that he adjusted his grip on the overnight bag he carried. She wondered when he had gotten the bag.

"I know what you're thinking, Nancy, but I

don't normally walk out on women in the middle of dinner. It really was urgent business. I probably should have told you, but I just didn't want to take any chances."

He drew her aside to a little alcove where no one could overhear them. "The thing is," he said softly, "I got a call from one of the kidnappers, saying I was to meet with him in Chicago."

"Then why the fancy escape?" Nancy asked. "Why couldn't I drive you there?"

"He made it clear I was to come alone." David looked at her intently. "And I knew it would be a lot faster if I flew. So I took a commuter flight there, only to find that I had been set up. No one contacted me at the meeting place they'd arranged."

"I see," Nancy said. "So your famous second sight failed you in this case."

LeGrand winced. "I guess so, Nancy. It happens to the best of us on occasion."

"Oh, well," Nancy said, "I forgive you. I can't stay mad at my favorite psychic." They started walking again, and Nancy said, "Do you need a ride back to your hotel?"

"That would be great. I turned in my rental car at the airport—last night."

As he followed Nancy to the parking lot and her waiting car, David said, "I'm relieved Sharon turned up and is okay."

"Me, too," Nancy agreed. She took the driver's

seat, and David got in beside her. Then he reached across and put his overnight bag on the backseat.

Before starting the engine, Nancy turned to him. "Well, do you want to hear what I've been up to while you were gone?" she asked, giving him a mischievous grin.

"Definitely!" he said. "Knowing you, I'm sure you weren't just sitting around."

"Well, it's not what you probably think," Nancy said. "Actually, I got inspired by you."

"Me? I don't understand. . . ."

Nancy shrugged. "Normally, I wouldn't have paid any attention to a lead like this. But you've convinced me there is such a thing as ESP."

"Don't tell me you've been getting vibrations yourself," David said, really smiling now.

"Not exactly," Nancy said. "You know my friend Bess, though? She's really into this psychic—Madame Tatiana Dove. Do you know her?"

"Ha! Do I know her? Nancy, she's the biggest joke on the professional circuit. Have you ever met the woman? She's totally ridiculous!"

"That's what I thought, too," Nancy told him. "I mean, the feathers and the beads and all. . . ."

"Exactly," David said.

"But then she predicted two things that actually happened later. She knew about Sharon's disappearance before the papers reported it—"

"That's easy," David scoffed. "There are lots of ways to find out about things like that."

". . . and she knew about the note in the sleeve of Sharon's jacket." Nancy gave him a meaningful look. "Maybe it's just a coincidence, I don't know. Maybe she's as crazy as she seems. But I got a call from her this morning, telling me to come over right away—she claims to have important information about Sharon's kidnapping."

"What?" Nancy noticed that David was starting to get anxious now. "Nancy, surely you don't take anything this woman says seriously?"

"Oh, I do," Nancy assured him. "And I'm sure you will, too, once you've heard what she has to say. You see, we've got a photograph of the kidnapper, and Madame's gotten strong vibrations from it."

Nancy fished out of her pocket a cropped photocopy of the news photo she'd found in the library. This version showed only the head of LeGrand's assistant, enlarged to twice the original's size. She'd had it made before leaving for the airport.

There was a brief moment of silence, but David recovered quickly. "This is him?" he asked. "I thought he had a scar. Didn't you say he did?"

"It was phony," Nancy explained.

"Where did you get this photo?" David asked.

"That's just it," Nancy told him. "Madame Tatiana gave it to me. And it's him, all right. I'd swear to it in court."

Nancy started the car, and minutes later they pulled up outside Madame's building. Nancy noticed that David LeGrand had the air of a wary tiger as he went inside with her. He was still carrying his overnight bag. It was odd that he hadn't left it in the car, Nancy noted. She thought she knew what was inside—and she meant to find out for sure.

Madame was waiting for them, with Bess by her side. Bess nodded quickly to Nancy to indicate she'd made all the preparations.

Madame greeted David LeGrand with disdain, and the feeling was obviously mutual. "Well?" David said. "What's this important information you have?"

"I know the identities of the kidnappers of Sharon Krane," Madame said, raising one eyebrow.

"I see." David smirked. "Did the cards tell you?"

Madame just looked back at him, silently.

"By the way, where did you manage to come by that photograph?" he challenged her. "He's an unsavory-looking guy."

"He's your former assistant," Nancy said bluntly.

At the same moment Madame bent over a

large crystal ball on the table. "Mr. LeGrand," she said, "I wonder if you see what I see in the ball."

David went over to the table. Madame Tatiana had placed the news photo of David with his assistants between the ball and the base on which it sat. She turned on a light in the base. The photo and caption were clearly visible in the crystal ball.

"What is this?" David asked, taking a step backward. "Some kind of trick?"

"Do you recognize the picture, David?" Nancy asked.

"Of course not!" he said hotly. "Look, I've had thousands of photos taken of me. This guy certainly was never one of my assistants, I can tell you that. That was probably just somebody hanging around to get an autograph!"

Nancy caught Madame's eye and slyly indicated the overnight bag. Suddenly Madame Tatiana began to sway and moan. "Check his bag!" Madame intoned, pointing to it.

"David?" Nancy said, turning her gaze to him.

"This is preposterous!" he sputtered. "I'm not going to play along anymore with this crazy woman!"

"What's the matter?" Nancy asked. "You're not afraid to show us what's in your bag, are you?"

"I . . . um, of course not," David said, managing a mirthless laugh. "Go ahead and look."

Nancy unzipped the bag and reached her hand in. She came out holding a fistful of insulin vials.

"It's not what you think," David said, his composure back to normal. "I got those vials in Chicago to bring to the kidnappers, in the hope that it would help prolong Sharon's life! You can have the lot numbers checked if you like, Nancy. They won't match the ones stolen the other night. In fact, I had to get them from a diabetic friend who happened to have enough to spare."

"Very touching," Nancy said dryly, dropping the insulin vials into her own bag.

"Nancy, I can't believe this!" David protested. "It's like you're suddenly a different person."

"I'm not the one who's been living a lie," Nancy shot back. "And if you're as innocent as you say you are, let us into your hotel suite so we can check for evidence."

"Listen," David warned her, "I can't be pushed around like this. If you think you can just come barging into my hotel room and tear it apart because of some crazy theory of yours—do you realize who you're dealing with?"

"I think I do," Nancy said calmly. "Now, are you going to take us on a tour of your suite, or do I have to get a warrant? As soon as I tell Captain Krane I've found insulin vials on you, he'll get a warrant instantly."

David LeGrand stood there, thinking. Nancy was sure he was calculating whether or not to let her in and take a chance his assistant had cleaned things up. She knew he wouldn't want a police search team in there, with all their sophisticated equipment. She was betting—and hoping—he'd take a chance on her.

He did. "All right, come on," he said.

Fifteen minutes later he was opening the door to his suite. Nancy noted the Do Not Disturb sign on the door. That was probably to keep the maid out, Nancy thought. She, Bess, George, and Madame Tatiana filed into the room. The suite was clean and smelled of cleaning fluid. Nancy sniffed. There was also a hint of paint thinner in the air. To get dye off skin? she wondered.

The room was large and comfortably furnished. Nancy went straight over to the bed. It had been made but not professionally.

Nancy searched the room while Bess and David watched. This would probably have been where David's accomplice tried to give Sharon her insulin shot, Nancy thought, the place with the "comfortable bed."

Where was that broken vial? Nancy checked the wastebaskets, under the bed, everywhere. Nothing. Nor did she see any traces of dye when she turned out the lights and flicked on her flashlight.

"Well?" LeGrand asked, sitting on the bed. "Satisfied?"

Nancy frowned. Was there anyplace she'd overlooked? She closed her eyes and tried to picture the scene. . . . Sharon lying on the bed, sick and thrashing, the man with the scar trying to give her an injection with the last good vial of insulin. . . . Sharon's arm knocking into his, making him drop the vial. . . . He would have picked up the broken glass. But what if he'd missed some?

Nancy got down and looked under the bed again. The man with the scar would have done the same. Then she felt behind one of the bed's wheels and . . .

"Bingo!" Nancy came up with a small piece of glass. On it was stamped the last three digits of a lot number. Nancy was pretty sure she knew where it came from.

"Bess," she said triumphantly as David Le-Grand's face fell, "call Captain Krane and tell him to get over here right away. We've found our kidnapper!"

A few days later, after the partial lot number on the insulin vial Nancy'd found had been matched to the stolen insulin, David LeGrand confessed to the kidnapping of Sharon Krane. His accomplice was picked up in Chicago, and also confessed.

Chief McGinnis had told Nancy that the two men, dressed as hotel maintenance staff, had moved the unconscious Sharon to David's suite inside a laundry cart. The assistant had indeed panicked when Sharon went into her diabetic coma. After being arrested, he panicked even more. In addition to implicating David in the other two kidnappings, he told Chicago police that David had sent him to River Heights to check out places to hide whoever they kidnapped. He also said that they had kidnapped Sharon because she had been an easy target—she was out walking alone at night. David LeGrand had been furious when he learned that Sharon was a cop's daughter.

For his part, David said that he had never intended to take the money. He had planned to "solve" the case before the night the money was to be dropped off. But because of Sharon's condition, he had gone to Chicago to get insulin. His assistant, he said, had gotten greedy and decided to steal the money for himself.

"How did you know it was David, Nan?" Bess asked Nancy when she finished recounting the story. The two girls, along with George and Sharon Krane, were treating themselves to ice-cream sundaes at Scoops, a local ice-cream parlor. Sharon, of course, was having the sugarless version.

"I didn't know for sure," Nancy confessed. "I

only had a hunch that if we spooked David and threw him off balance, he'd lose his cool and make a mistake. And he did. He let us into his hotel room."

"Hunches?" George teased. "Sounds like you've bought into the supernatural after all."

"Come on, George," Nancy protested. "It's all logic and deduction, that's all."

"Yeah, right," Bess said with a knowing smile. 'Admit it, Nan. You were wrong. There *is* such a thing as second sight—and Madame has it."

"I don't know about second sight," Nancy said, "but I will admit, Madame was pretty impressive. I'll never figure out how she knew about the note in Sharon's jacket sleeve."

"You ought to become a clairvoyant yourself, the way you found that piece of the insulin vial," Bess said.

"Hmmm," Nancy said, raising an eyebrow at her friend and giving her a dramatic look. "Maybe I should, Bess. Maybe I should. . . ."

Nancy's next case:

Nancy, Bess, and George have come to Chicago for a weekend of shopping and a night out at a trendy new restaurant owned by Adam Sledge, lead singer of the chart-busting band Void. The place is the coolest thing going, packed with celebs and pulsating with excitement—a wild scene that gets even wilder when a smoke bomb goes off!

Behind the scenes Nancy turns up a slew of suspects and all the ingredients for danger: jealousy, greed, revenge. But perhaps most dangerous of all is Adam Sledge. The rock star's putting all the moves on Nancy, and he's proving to be a major distraction. If she fails to focus on the investigation, someone could get seriously hurt, including herself . . . in *Skipping a Beat,* Case #117 in The Nancy Drew Files™.

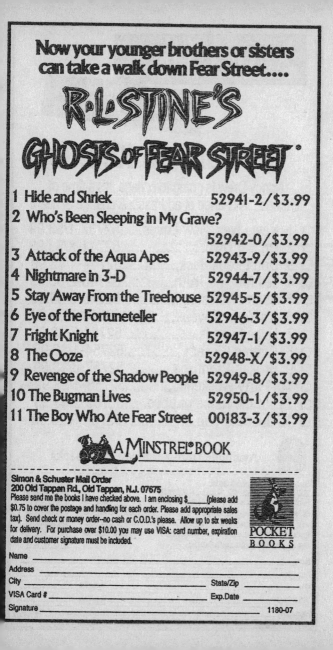